P9-CAO-685

To The Wonderful Stud[ents]
and Intelligent
at I C S,
Best Wishes
and historically yours,
Christine Petrell
Kallevig

(04-16-03)

Carry me home Cuyahoga : a
historic novel /
3620001749198

CARRY ME HOME
CUYAHOGA

A Historical Novel

Christine Petrell Kallevig

Illustrations by Jeanette Bill-Cole

Iroquois Community School LMC
District 62
Des Plaines, Illinois

International
P. O. Box 470505, Broadview Heights, Ohio 44147

Text copyright © 1996 by Christine Petrell Kallevig.
Illustrations copyright © 1995 by Jeanette Bill-Cole.

All rights reserved. No part of this book may be reproduced,
transmitted or utilized in any form or by any means, electronic or
mechanical, including photocopying, recording or by any information storage and retrieval system, without permission in writing
from the Publisher:

Storytime Ink International
P. O. Box 470505
Broadview Heights, Ohio 44147
(216) 838-4881

ISBN 0-9628769-7-6 (trade paper)
ISBN 0-9628769-8-4 (limited edition hard cover)

First Edition
10 9 8 7 6 5 4 3 2 1
Printed in the United States of America.

Library of Congress Catalog Card Number 95-072499

ACKNOWLEDGMENTS

Copyrighted Photograph of Lorenzo Carter on page 102 reprinted
with written permission from the Western Reserve Historical
Society, Cleveland, Ohio.

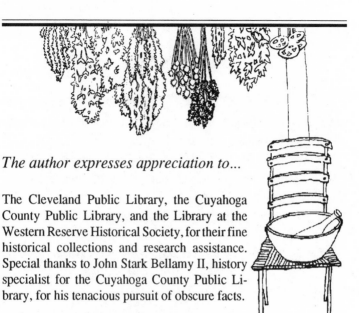

The author expresses appreciation to...

The Cleveland Public Library, the Cuyahoga County Public Library, and the Library at the Western Reserve Historical Society, for their fine historical collections and research assistance. Special thanks to John Stark Bellamy II, history specialist for the Cuyahoga County Public Library, for his tenacious pursuit of obscure facts.

Andrea Mitchell, Curator of Educational Programs at the Cleveland African American Museum; Edward Jay Pershey, Ph.D., Director of Education at the Western Reserve Historical Society; Randall McShepard, Assistant Director of Program Development for the Cleveland Bicentennial Commission; William Donohue Ellis, author of *Early Settlers of Cleveland;* Robert Wheeler, Ph.D., co-author of *Cleveland: A Concise History;* Nicolaus Heun, David L. Kallevig, and Carol Gallatin for encouraging readings and valuable editorial input.

The knowledgeable staff at Hale Farm & Village in Bath, Ohio, a part of the Western Reserve Historical Society, for demonstrating pioneer crafts, techniques, and culture.

Author's Note

Carry Me Home Cuyahoga is a historical novel. Although its conversations and descriptions are imaginary, all of its characters actually lived in or near Cleveland, Ohio in March through December of 1806, and most of the events occurring in the story were based on accounts obtained from historical documents. The following books were especially helpful in this research:

Early History of Cleveland, Ohio with Biographical Notices of the Pioneers and Surveyors by Charles Whittlesey, written in 1867.

Early Settlers of Cleveland by William Donohue Ellis, written in 1976.

History of Cuyahoga County, Ohio In Three Parts, by Crisfield Johnson, written in 1879.

Incidents of Pioneer Life in the Early Settlement of the Connecticut Western Reserve, by Harvey Rice, written in 1881.

Indians of the Cuyahoga Valley and Vicinity, by Virginia Chase Bloetscher, written in 1980.

Memorable Negroes In Cleveland's Past, by Russell H. Davis, written in 1969.

Pioneer Families of Cleveland, Vol. 1 by Gertrude Van Rensselaer Wickham, written in 1914.

Chapters

©Bill-Cole '95

1

LANDSLIDE

"Henry Carter, this is your last warning! Sit still or you'll answer to the switch!" Master Adams glared at the restless nine-year-old from his table near the schoolhouse hearth.

"Oh yes, sir! You won't have to tell me no more!"

"ANY more, Henry. Tell you ANY more."

"Yes, sir. That's just what I said. I'll sit still as long as this here bench sits still." He held his breath and stiffened his back, awkwardly freezing himself in mid-wiggle.

The split-log bench Henry shared with the other boys squeaked every time he squirmed, and although he tried his hardest, he couldn't stop squirming – and squeaking – not when he had two special secrets to protect! One was hidden beneath his linsey-woolsey pants and the other, in a lumpy knot at the bottom edge of his homespun shirt.

The first secret was his big brother's doing. Alonzo, who was sixteen and too old for school, had convinced him to slip a piece of buckskin under his pants. The jagged bench had slivered his bottom for four days straight during this, his first week of school. Digging out hickory splinters with a blistering hot darning needle was definitely not the kind of homework he ever wanted to do!

Alonzo's plan was working. Henry's bottom felt much better, but the unattached leather kept sliding down the legs of his stretchy breeches. As soon as he tugged it up from one side, whoops, it was falling down the other. With all that slipping and sliding going on inside his pants, Henry couldn't possibly think about his lesson.

Master Adams wanted him to write correctly about where he lived, so Henry had to practice over and over until he learned to spell every word: *I live at the mouth of the Cuyahoga River in Cleveland in Geauga County in Ohio in the United States of America. I live at the....*

It hardly makes sense, he thought, to live in all those different places at the same time. Anyway, his father claimed that Ohio was going to break up Geauga County and give Cleveland its own county pretty soon. Henry told Master Adams that practicing Geauga was a stupid, no-account, useless waste of time, but for some unknown reason, his teacher made him do it anyway.

Henry sighed and straightened the buckskin again. He looked up into cold hostile eyes.

"Excuse me, sir. I won't move no more."

"ANY more..."

"Yes, sir. I don't mean to be no trouble."

"ANY trouble..."

"Yes, sir. My father says that we should help you as much as we can. My legs was stiffening up, was all."

"WERE stiffening, Henry. Say it correctly, please."

2

"Yes, sir. They was aching."

The new schoolmaster, fresh from Connecticut and still wearing real leather boots and a tailor-made suit, leaped to his feet. His bench toppled over and just missed falling into the fire. Henry snickered, but the other children pretended not to notice as they sat facing the walls where writing shelves were balanced on pegs jutting out of the logs.

Master Adams huffed and slapped an open hand against his rough-hewn table, risking a sliver of his own.

"Your legs WERE aching, Mr. Carter."

"Yes, sir. They sure was. But they're better, now, thank you. We was sitting here a long time, was all."

"WERE! They sure WERE! We WERE sitting here a long time!"

"Yes, sir. We sure was and I know that we most definitely agree about it, too."

Henry tucked a loose strand of long straight hair into the knot fastened at the back of his neck. His dark brow furrowed with confusion as he peeked at the bundle of willow switches on his teacher's table. Maybe his father had been right about the new schoolmaster. He hid a smile as he remembered Master Adam's arrival just last week.

"I wonder how long that fancy pants is going to last?" Major Lorenzo Carter had speculated when he had first laid eyes on the young man from Connecticut. The hunting dogs tied outside the Carter barn were warning that a stranger had arrived.

"Can't have much sense if he traveled the Lake Erie

Trail all by himself at this time of year," the rugged pioneer had muttered to his wife and five children who were all busy with midday chores.

Henry dropped an armful of kindling by the stone fireplace that formed the center wall of their spacious cabin. "Isn't March the worst time for the lake route?" he had asked.

His father nodded briskly. "You're right, Henry. Lake Erie is deadly in early spring. The freezing head winds and choppy water make it near impossible to paddle a canoe west from Buffalo."

"It's still too cold and muddy to drive an ox team across land," said Alonzo. At sixteen, he was the oldest of the Carter children and already six feet tall like their father.

"But not cold enough for a sleigh on the shore ice," added Henry as he stacked the kindling into a tidy pile.

"He must have walked from Buffalo," concluded the Major. "That's almost two hundred miles."

"Is he hurt?" asked seven-year-old Polly. She was patiently pumping the handle of a wooden butter churn. The only trait she shared with her two rowdy brothers and her two spirited sisters was their father's coloring of dark eyes and dark hair. Quiet and careful like their mother, Polly worried about everything. Her brothers and sisters worried about nothing.

"Not that I can tell," said the Major, his sharp eyes studying the newcomer. "I hope he stays for a while, fancy pants and all. Cleveland needs a school teacher to bring in more settlers. A half dozen families aren't enough for a

4

real town."

Alonzo stood shoulder to shoulder with his father and shook his head with disdain. "We were with the first families to move here, and we waited until May to make the crossing. Even Moses Cleaveland and the Connecticut Land Company had enough sense to wait for decent weather before sending their surveyors. I wonder why Henry and Polly's new teacher is so eager to get here?"

"No doubt he feels the same as I did back in 1797, son," reflected the Major. "Once you decide to make a new life for yourself, you can't hardly wait to get started. I owned a few acres in Vermont, but not enough to really prosper. I wanted more for your mother and for you children. Your Uncle Ezekiel and I visited the Cuyahoga Valley before we decided to move, but most likely our new school teacher relied on the ads from the Connecticut Land Company."

"Cheap land! Great opportunities!" quoted Henry with a grin.

"Cheap land! Cheap land!" sang two-year-old Mercy, the youngest Carter child. Her chubby fingers struggled to wind up a ball of yarn.

"Is our land cheap?" asked Polly.

The Major snorted. "Not near cheap enough. There's so much land for sale in the rest of Ohio that no one wants to settle up here on Lake Erie."

"You can't hardly blame them, Lorenzo," said Mrs. Carter from her spinning wheel. "Our nine years here haven't been easy."

His fiery black eyes softened when he looked at his frail wife. "We would have been worse off in Vermont trying to scratch a living from that little farm. You know that, Rebecca. We have much more here – the tavern, the ferry service, good Indian trading, plenty of land, and as much game as we can eat..."

"And the worst roads in Ohio," she added.

"You can't hardly call our old Indian trails roads, Mother," said Alonzo.

"The Connecticut Land Company does," she said, working the spinning wheel even faster than before.

"More settlers would come if it was easier to get here," agreed Laura, the Carter's oldest daughter. She was using the light from the window to sew tiny stitches into the sleeve of a new towcloth shirt. "It's not so bad in Cleveland – if you can get used to the Indians, that is," she added.

"And if you like wolves eating your hogs," said Henry with a grin.

"And coons and deer destroying your crops," said Alonzo. "If only the fevers – "

"Hush about the fevers!" barked the Major. His angular face hardened into an expression of stubborn determination.

"I won't allow any talk about unhealthy air, especially under my own roof!" he commanded. "And anyway, the fevers only bother the weak and puny and ill-prepared..."

"Is the new school teacher weak and puny and ill-prepared?" Polly asked meekly.

"Not if he just walked two hundred miles through mud

6

and slush," said Alonzo. "His coat and boots still look new! And look at that fancy shirt!"

"If he survives through the summer, he'll switch to homespun and moccasins like everyone else," growled the Major.

"Is he smart enough to teach us?" Polly asked, her dark eyes deeply concerned.

"We'll find out in time, little rabbit," said her father, patting her head.

"If he doesn't have sense," she persisted, "will we have to go back to now-and-again lessons with Mother and Laura?"

"Father said that we'll have to find out!" said Henry in his bossy big-brother voice. "And anyway, who cares? We don't have no use for book learning no how."

"Not true, Henry!" snapped the Major as he opened the door to calm his dogs. "The Cleveland settlement needs a school teacher so we are going to help him as much as we can, whether we have use for book learning or not!"

Henry hid in the loft while his father invited Master Adams in for a meal of corn bread and venison stew. He had been relieved when his teacher declined his father's offer to lodge in their cabin, which doubled as a tavern.

Master Adams began teaching right away. His first week in Cleveland had felt like the longest week of Henry's life. Despite the slivers, Henry had tried his hardest to sit still and concentrate on spelling and numbers. Unlike Polly, who loved school and preferred to be inside, Henry just knew he would die if he had to control his energy for even one more day. Fortunately, the first thunderstorm of 1806 happened, just in time to give him a great idea for his second secret, a sure-fire way to make school much more exciting.

The storm had roared in off of Lake Erie the night before, just after the last splinter had been wrenched from Henry's backside.

"After the hard winter we've had," Mrs. Carter had said, "we can thank the Lord that he's bringing us rain instead of snow."

"I'll thank him tomorrow when I see that the river's not flooded," the Major had muttered.

Then a log in the fire popped louder than usual.

"That reminds me of that time a couple years ago when we were overrun by those Ottawa Indian braves," said Alonzo, his wide smile glowing in an eerie reflection of the dancing firelight. "You remember, Laura. They fell asleep on the floor after drinking too much of Bryant's firewater."

Laura laughed, her pretty face hidden in the shadows of the dark cabin. At fourteen, she was blossoming into an independent pioneer woman, already taller and stronger than her mother.

"How could I forget?" she asked. "They all seemed to drop dead, right where they were standing. One minute they were asking for more food, and the next, they were out cold on the floor."

"How many were there?" asked Henry.

"About a dozen," said Laura. "And that was about a

dozen too many for me."

"I don't remember any of this," said the Major.

"That's because you were away on Ohio militia business," said Alonzo. "It was one of the first times you left me in charge of the tavern."

"I don't remember it, either," said Mrs. Carter.

"You were resting in the back room with little Mercy, Mother," said Laura. "Don't you remember how fussy Mercy was back then? She cried all day, every day. By the time the Ottawa braves were on the floor, you had finally quieted her down. Henry and Polly were asleep in the loft, and Alonzo and I had to figure out a way to make the sleeping Indians leave. Otherwise, we'd have to take turns staying awake all night to watch the tavern."

"What did you do?" asked Henry.

"I was getting pretty fed up," said Alonzo, "so I kicked some chestnuts into the fire. Before you knew it, the nuts began to sizzle. And then they exploded, hitting the Ottawa braves like red-hot bullets."

"You should have seen them spring up!" laughed Laura. "They were reeling and falling over each other, all set to defend themselves. I thought they'd take our scalps."

"But they were too sleepy to think straight," said Alonzo. "Maybe they thought the fire spirits were attacking, because they ran outside to take cover behind the trees. We bolted the door, swept up the rest of the chestnuts, and climbed up into the attic to go to sleep."

"My bed never felt so good," said Laura.

"Did Mercy wake up and cry again?" Polly asked,

worried as usual.

"No, and you can be sure that we kept the rest of the nuts away from the fire so she wouldn't," said Alonzo.

"Mercy no cry baby," whined the sturdy toddler.

"You were then, honey. A long time ago when you didn't know better," her mother murmured as she stroked Mercy's thick black hair. Her weary eyes were sad when she asked, "Didn't this happen after Baby Rebecca and Lorenzo Junior died in August and September? We were all so sick that year."

Laura nodded. "Yes, we'd just moved into this cabin. Wasn't that about the same time that Amos Spafford used a hoe to kill a bear over on Water Street?" she asked Alonzo.

"No, I think we were still in our old cabin under the hill when that happened," he said. "The thing I remember the most about the year Baby Rebecca and Lorenzo Junior died was how much Mercy cried. She was the loudest baby in Ohio!"

"Mercy big girl," pouted the indignant two-year-old. "Mercy no cry baby. Polly little bunny. Mercy big."

Polly protested while the others smiled and leaned closer together, the hypnotic flames reflected in their shining eyes. The inky blackness of the surrounding room deepened while the storm ravaged the brittle and leafless trees of the dense forest around them. The booming thunder and clattering hail stones were scary, but the sounds of branches snapping and waves crashing were even worse.

10

Henry needed something else to think about. "Did anything else happen because of the chestnuts?" he asked, hoping for another story.

"The next day, we heard that the Ottawa Indians were never coming back to our tavern," Laura said.

"Yes," laughed Alonzo. "They said that our chimney was cursed with evil spirits."

"Did they go in the woods and have a White Dog Feast to bring them better luck?" asked Henry.

Alonzo shrugged. "I doubt it. The Senecas have White Dog Feasts, not the Ottawas. Isn't that right, Father?"

The Major nodded. "I don't know anyone who would sacrifice a white dog to the Great Manitou just because he got hit by some hot nuts," he said with a rare smile.

Henry had laughed long and hard as he imagined the sleepers awakened and startled by the exploding nuts, but then an even funnier picture popped into his head. What would his fancy pants schoolmaster do if evil spirits suddenly invaded the chimney in the new schoolhouse?

He could hardly wait to find out! That morning, when he followed Alonzo's advice and hid the buckskin in his pants, he also grabbed a handful of dry chestnuts from the dwindling supply that he and Polly had gathered back in October. He knotted them into the bottom edge of his gray homespun shirt and waited impatiently to start the fireworks. His chance had finally come!

Master Adams, disgusted with Henry's bad grammar, aimed his steely gaze at Polly's side of the room. Just as Henry hoped, the Connecticut man clasped his hands behind his back and strutted across to the younger children. As soon as he stooped to look at Polly's work, Henry unknotted his second secret and threw the whole handful of chestnuts into the fire. Only his friend Almon Kingsbury, who hiked five miles to school from Newburgh, saw the nuts fly in. The boys flashed excited grins and pretended to study their spelling lesson.

When nothing happened, Henry's face turned red. *I should've tried it out at home last night while Alonzo and Laura told their story about the Ottawa braves. Maybe they were just pulling my leg... Maybe the nuts won't even explode...*

Finally, after what seemed like forever, a crackling sizzle sputtered in the fire. The boys smiled and braced themselves for action. But then barking and gunfire erupted outside.

"Everyone clear out of the schoolhouse!" someone shouted. Another gun was fired, a signal that something important was happening.

"Get out! The hill fell into the lake! The school might be next!"

The children charged for the door in a disorderly heap, nearly trampling Master Adams. Henry ran to the window, but he only saw shadows through the greased paper that substituted for glass in the square opening.

"Hurry, Henry. Let's find out what's happening!" shouted Master Adams.

Henry had no choice. With a long backwards glance toward the fire, he allowed himself to be ushered outside.

Alonzo and Major Carter, surrounded by children and excited dogs, were pointing at Lake Erie when Henry and his teacher joined them.

"Two hundred feet of shoreline disappeared!" shouted Alonzo. "Amos Spafford's hired man was plowing on the hill. He chained his oxen to a tree and went home to eat lunch, but when he came back, the beasts were gone! He looked over the edge, and there they were, still attached to the tree, chewing their cuds as though nothing had happened. But the ground sank away, taking the tree and plow and oxen with it!"

"It was because of the storm last night," added the Major. "I told Spafford that the earth was too wet to turn over. The waves smashed the shoreline and caved it in. Lake Erie and the Cuyahoga River will wash away the whole town if we don't take care and plow at the right time."

While everyone else pushed to get a better look at the sunken oxen and fallen tree, Henry removed his deerskin cushion and returned to the schoolhouse just as a burning chestnut blazed across the room.

At any other time, Henry would have been as excited as everyone else about the missing shoreline. But not now, not at the very moment that his greatest prank was working out so well! Imagine! Upstaged by a landslide! What could possibly go wrong next?

1 inch = 125 miles

HURON

LAKE ONTARIO

Niagara Falls, Ontario

Buffalo

NEW

Detroit

LAKE ERIE

Cleveland

PENNSYLVANI

Pittsburgh

OHIO

MAR

★ Columbus

Washington D.C.

1 inch = 4 miles

Lake Erie

Doans Corners

Indian Mound

Carter's Tavern

Carter's
Corn Field

Ben's
Wreck

Rocky
R.

Cuyahoga
R.

Newburgh

Approximate population in 1806

Cleveland	46
Doans Corners/Newburgh	131
Cincinnati	2,500
Columbus (not founded until 1812)	
Ohio	90,000
Pittsburgh	3,100
Washington D. C.	12,000
United States	6,451,000

Cuyahoga is an Indian name for
"Crooked River"

Tinkers
Creek

Ben's Hut

14

RESCUE

Five days later, a gusty March wind blew in from Lake Erie. Henry and Polly were at school and Major Carter had gone hunting with his dogs. Laura helped her mother bake corn bread in the oven that was built into their broad stone chimney, while little Mercy made a pussy-willow house for her favorite rag doll. Alonzo had just finished clearing the fallen trees from last week's storm. He trotted down to the river to check that his father's ferry boat was well secured in the rising water.

The extra run-off from the storm caused early flooding in a river already swollen from a winter of heavy snowfall. The Cuyahoga River mouth, usually a shallow swamp, was now swift and murky as flood waters washed top soil and tree limbs into the turbulent waves of Lake Erie. Alonzo tightened the boat line and stared wide-eyed at the current, mesmerized by its constant swirls and ripples. His gaze followed the bloated corpse of a drown hog as it bobbed along toward the massive lake.

That's one the wolves didn't get, he thought. At the point where the muddy river began to mix with the clear blue lake, he was surprised to see that a canoe had turned in and was battling upstream against the current.

"Aye, Carter!" the paddlers shouted. "Pull us in. A man needs help!"

Two French trappers who had left Cleveland that morning for a long westward paddle to Detroit had unexpectedly returned. As their powerful strokes brought them closer, Alonzo saw a pair of dark, twitching hands dangling out from under the pile of Chippewa blankets that were stacked in the center of their canoe. They threw a rope to shore and leaned back while Alonzo pulled them over to the mucky river bank.

"Hurry, boy. We found a half frozen man west of here by the mouth of the Rocky River."

The first of the burly trappers hopped out while the paddler in back threaded his way through the sixteen foot dugout, deftly dodging the injured man who was sprawled face down over a bulging pack of trading goods. They pulled the canoe completely out of the river and without a word, peeled away the blankets, revealing the largest and blackest man that Alonzo had ever seen. His coffee-colored neck oozed with bloody cuts and Alonzo saw purple bruises through the remnants of his soaked and shredded clothing. His dark brown eyes rolled open, but they were glazed and unfocused. He moaned, too weak to raise himself out of the canoe.

With perfect teamwork, the trappers, one on each side, gently flipped him over and sat him up in a forward slouch. They linked their muscled hands under his knees and behind his shoulders, hoisting him out of the canoe and up the hill toward Carter's Tavern. Alonzo threw a blanket over him as he ran ahead to warn his mother.

"Mother! Laura! Get a bed ready by the fire. A man's been found by the Rocky River."

They grabbed some quilts and spread them on the wooden floor in front of the hearth.

"Put more wood in the fire, Alonzo," Rebecca Carter said, her face already flushed and sweating from baking.

"He's hurt bad, Mother."

"I'll get my herbs," she said, but gasped with surprise when the trappers barged through the door. They were straining and didn't look like they could take ten more steps without dropping their delirious passenger.

"My Lord in Heaven, he's an African! Won't your father be surprised! Lay him down and take off those wet clothes. Laura, start some bath water. We have to clean those cuts. And we'll need some broth. Watch where you throw those rags, now. Put them out the door, Alonzo."

Laura carried the water buckets outside while Rebecca hurried into the back room for her healing herbs. The trappers unsheathed their long curved knives and sliced off what was left of his tattered layers of wool and leather. They covered him with dry blankets and struggled to pull off his boots. After much tugging and twisting, the injured man groaned and fainted dead away as the boots and socks finally came off. The Frenchmen gasped, their eyes wide with horror, when they saw the reason the boots had been so tight.

"The frost has taken his toes," one of them muttered, his bearded lips twisted with disgust. He held his breath and turned his face away from the horrible stench that suddenly filled the cabin. His partner coughed and shielded his nose, hastily discarding the boots as they both backed away.

Rebecca came back with her herb basket, but she, too, was sickened by the over-powering smell. The man's injuries were too gruesome. She dashed outside, unable to stop her stomach from emptying right then and there, just as Laura returned with the water.

She dropped the buckets and glanced at the man's rotted toes. "Alonzo, get rid of those boots and see that Mother is all right," she said. "And while you're outside, bring me her herbs."

Laura had never looked more like her father as her intelligent eyes examined the dark stranger. "Whatever you do," she said, pinching her nose, "*don't* close the door."

Alonzo nodded and hurried outside. The trappers stumbled after him, eager to get away. They waited awkwardly by the barn until Rebecca regained her composure and looked up at them.

"Adieu, Madame Carter. We leave again for Detroit," they said, bowing politely and averting their eyes away from her distress.

"Yes, God be with you," she said weakly. Pale and trembling, she wiped her mouth with her apron bib and waved good-bye.

"We'll fix him up, good as new!" Alonzo called after them. "Stop to see us on your return trip. You won't be sorry that you brought him back!"

Anxious to make up for lost travel time, the Frenchmen nearly collided with Major Carter as they slid back down the muddy path to the river. His hunting dogs barked and jumped playfully, excited by their romp in the woods.

"I saw your canoe. Back for more rum?" the Major asked, but his smile disappeared when he saw their somber faces.

"What's wrong? What's happened?"

The Frenchmen nudged the dogs away and nodded back toward the cabin. "We brought back a man we found clinging to a tree by the mouth of Rocky River," said one of them.

"He's a giant, but barely alive," explained the other. "We couldn't get a word out of him. We don't know where he came from or why he was marooned. We didn't see anyone else and there was no sign of a wrecked boat."

The first trapper looked down, embarrassed. "I don't want to tell you this, Monsieur Carter, but I fear that his huge size and terrible injuries were too much for Madame. Probably even too much for you, Monsieur. Only a miracle can save him, now!"

The Major didn't wait for any more of the story. He ran up to the cabin and arrived just as Polly and Henry were getting home from school.

"Rebecca!" he shouted. "Are you all right?"

He leaned his rifle against a tree stump and put his

large hands on his wife's narrow shoulders, turning her toward him, looking steadily into her eyes.

"We'll be needing Anna Gun," she said softly.

Major Carter released his wife and spun toward Henry and Polly. "Henry! Go up to the ridge and fetch Mrs. Gun! Tell her to bring her best healing medicines. Hurry! We have a man in bad trouble!"

Henry never questioned his father when he used that tone of voice. It meant do as your told and don't ask why. He turned and ran up the path that led to Newburgh, a cluster of cabins about five miles uphill from Cleveland. If he hurried, he'd be able to join Almon Kingsbury and the other Newburgh children on their hike home from school.

"Polly!" continued the Major. "Go fetch Mercy and keep her away from the cabin. Don't go near the river, and stay away from that no-good crowd gathered at Bryant's still. You both stay outside until someone calls you in!"

Her large brown eyes nervously shifted to her mother's face in search of reassurance or an explanation. But Rebecca only nodded firmly to her daughter and turned back to the cabin. Polly found Mercy playing over by the barn, and quietly joined her pussy-willow game.

Alonzo had loosened the blanket around the unconscious stranger's shoulders and Laura was cleaning one of his arms when their parents returned.

The Major thrust his hands up with surprise. "Well, I'll be! No one told me he was an African!" he exclaimed, glaring at his wife. He slammed his rifle down on their large table and began to pace around the room, pulling off his deerskin coat and leggings, then tossing them aside.

"We've never had an African here before!" he ranted. "Can't say that I've ever been in the same room as one. Used to see a few when I was a boy in Warren, Connecticut. That was before the Quakers put a stop to slave owning on those old dairy farms in Litchfield County. And I heard that Moses Cleaveland had an African guide him from New York. A freeman, I guess. Don't know what happened to him, though."

He slapped Alonzo on the back as he walked by. "He's the first colored man you've ever seen, ain't he, boy?"

"Yes, sir," said Alonzo. "And I can't hardly believe my eyes! He's as black as can be!" Alonzo shook his head with amazement. "I believe he's darker than the darkest Indians. You told me about Africans and all, but I never knew that a man could be *this* color."

"His hair is same as our's," said Laura as she gently dabbed a festering gash on his arm. They all spoke carefully when the Major was excited like this. His hot temper and tendency to fly into action were unpredictable, even to his family. And they all knew how much he hated surprises.

"That it is," the Major said, pausing just long enough to focus on the stranger's head. A strand of Laura's long black hair rested on his forehead.

"Same color, but we're not curled like that," Alonzo said.

Rebecca kneeled to clean a welt on his cheek. "I

wonder where he came from," she murmured. "Looks to be about thirty, or so. He's such a big man. I feared those trappers would break their backs carrying him in. Then we'd have a roomful of invalids, wouldn't we?"

She paused, searching his face for clues. "He's got good strong bones," she said. "He must have suffered terribly. I've never heard of anyone surviving in Lake Erie in March. But I believe he's going to make it, Lorenzo. It must be a miracle. God delivered him to us, so he's our charge, now. When he's better, we'll find out why God sent him here."

"He seems to be warming up," said Laura. "And he's breathing regular."

"The smell's not bad anymore," said Alonzo. "There must have been a dead animal in his boots."

Laura grimaced and shook her head. "No, Alonzo. Did you see his toes? How are we going to heal his feet, Mother?"

She shook her head helplessly. "I don't know. I've never seen living flesh be so rotten. I pray that Anna Gun knows what to do."

"What's wrong with his feet?" asked the major suspiciously. "Got leg irons on them? Is he a runaway slave?"

"There's no chains on him," said Rebecca.

"Well? What's the problem then?"

"You'd better see for yourself," she said gently.

He lifted the blankets. "Ach! God almighty!" he sputtered, coughing and jerking away.

"I don't know if I like him or not," he huffed. "Can't

be any worse than the rest of the good-for-nothing drifters who hang around here for months at a time. Slave or no slave, leg irons or not, the only thing I know for sure is that he's not going anywhere with feet as bad as those!"

The Major began to retrieve his hunting clothes from around the cabin. He stopped at the door and turned back toward his family.

"The man is hurting," he announced. "So we're going to do everything we can to help him, no matter who he is or where he came from, no questions asked. It's the only decent thing to do!"

He shouted for Alonzo to follow as he stomped outside. "Bring the sledge, son," he barked. "Get the dogs! We have to go after more deer. We'll be wanting the extra meat. If all goes well with your mother and Anna Gun, we'll have an extra mouth to feed for a long, long time."

3

CURSED

Henry was supposed to help Anna Gun. "Why can't Alonzo do it?" he complained.

"Your father needs him to fill those cracks in the barn," Rebecca said.

"And what about Laura? Why can't she help Mrs. Gun?"

"I need Laura in the kitchen and to help look after Mercy. Would you rather do the cooking?"

Henry's eyes widened. "That's even worse woman's work! What about Polly? She never has to do anything!"

"Are you trying to say that Polly is stronger than you, Henry Carter? Can she bring in bigger piles of firewood? Can she haul more water from the spring?" Rebecca smiled as Henry squirmed.

"Ah, shucks," he said. "What will I have to do?"

"Mostly fetch things," she said, rubbing his shoulder. "Laura and I will help with the healing. Anna might want you to sit with the man and keep him company, but mostly she'll need those big muscles of yours."

Henry stood a little taller and brushed her hand away.

"Will I have to miss school?"

"I'm afraid so," she said.

Henry brightened. "Well, if no one else can do it, I guess it won't be so bad..."

Anything, except maybe corn scraping or soap making, was better than having to sit still on the jagged schoolhouse benches all day. But Henry wasn't sure that he'd like taking orders from Anna Gun. She was older and tougher than his mother, and his friend Almon Kingsbury, claimed that she was a witch. The Kingsbury farm was close to the Gun cabin, and Almon said he heard strange singing coming from there all the time.

Henry thought it might be true because Anna Gun was always telling stories about sinister ghosts lurking in the woods and evil spirits flowing through the waters. She was especially superstitious about the Cuyahoga River and jabbered on and on about how it was cursed and so was anyone living next to it.

She stayed with the Carters for three days, all that she could spare away from her own large family. Her oldest daughter, Philena, was due to have her first baby any day, and although she was not confident that the mysterious stranger was going to survive, she couldn't stay any longer.

"I don't like it that he hasn't been alert, yet," she said to Henry and Laura as she gathered her herbs and leftover cake of flaxseed. "But I expect that if he's going to make it, he'll wake up hungrier than a bear in a day or two, maybe even this afternoon. He's lucky to be such a big fellow. He would have never survived the cold without all that extra size."

"I'm glad all his feverish thrashing about has stopped," said Laura.

"And all that moaning," added Henry. Between Anna Gun's spooky stories and the giant stranger's groans, Henry hadn't been sleeping very well these last three nights. His bed was in the loft, directly above the cabin's main room where the stranger lay on a bed roll next to the hearth.

"The main worry right now are those toes," Anna said as Rebecca brought her a basket of freshly baked Johnny cakes.

"Shall we keep wetting the flaxseed poultice?" asked Rebecca.

"Yes, with warm lime water, and be sure to check that the blackening doesn't start creeping up his feet."

"It's so hard to tell," said Rebecca. "I'm still not used to the color of his skin. What if his feet get worse and I don't even notice it?"

"Amputation, that's what," said Anna sternly. "And you'll have to get someone else to do it!"

"Do Africans heal the same as white folks?" asked Rebecca nervously.

Anna cackled. "Land's sake, woman, of course! The Lord made us all the same on the inside. You should know that by now, living so close to the Indians all these years."

Anna was like a big sister to Rebecca. Their families arrived in Cleveland at about the same time, in the spring of 1797. Anna was well known for her nursing skills, especially in midwifery and helping to combat the annual scourge of fevers and chills.

An involuntary shiver passed through the more delicate Rebecca as she examined the dark stranger. "Is there any hope that his toes will recover?" she asked.

Anna shook her head and frowned. "His is the worst case of frostbite that I've ever seen. The icy cold froze his toes right through the flesh, and then his wet socks swelled up inside his boots and did even more damage. The toes were frozen, squashed, and cut off from dry air. Finally they began to rot, like some old smelly carcass in the woods."

Both Henry and Laura paled and shuddered. They met their mother's worried eyes.

"Our corn is about gone, but can we send some venison home with you?" gushed Rebecca, her words spilling out too fast in her eagerness to change the subject.

The older woman chuckled as she slipped her bonnet over her wiry gray hair. "After what we've seen these last three days, dead meat is not what I want to carry back with me. I'd have a pack of wolves tracking me all the way to Newburgh. Thanks for the offer, though. We all know that we can count on the Major and his dogs to keep us all supplied with game until the early crops come in."

"I hope you'll take more bread," said Rebecca.

"Yes, honey, I'd be grateful for a little more. I won't have time to bake when I get home."

Rebecca took the basket and added more Johnny

cakes. "We'll send Henry with news if the man starts to talk," she said.

"That's good. I'm mighty curious about how he came to be washed up in Lake Erie."

"And you send word about Philena's baby. Soon you'll be a grandmother, Anna. We'll have to start calling you Granny Gun."

"I like the sound of that, but Lord knows it's a struggle to feed another one."

"At least you're away from the fevers up there on the ridge," said Rebecca sadly.

"You're remembering the lost babies, aren't you? Well, one of these days, the Major will come to his senses and move you away from the river, too."

"Never."

"That man's more stubborn than a stump of oakwood."

Laura and Henry exchanged looks of wonderment. Anna Gun was the only person they knew who got away with saying such things about their father.

"He believes that if he deserts Cleveland and the Cuyahoga River, then everything he's worked so hard for will be lost," said Rebecca defensively. "He'll be thirty-nine this year, same as me, and he doesn't want to start all over from scratch. Anyway, he's been right about the opportunities down here, especially now that we own that extra land on the west side of the river. He says he has to stay in Cleveland to lure in new settlers and show them that it's possible to prosper."

"Prosper he has, but how many Lorenzo Carters are

there in the world?" scoffed the older woman. "You have to be half bear and half ox to survive the fevers. You're a lucky woman to have a man like him, but mark my words, the Cuyahoga River is cursed. It will bring you nothing but death and misery, Rebecca. Join us up on the ridge before it's too late."

Rebecca wrapped a protective arm around both Laura and Henry and smiled gently at her friend. "Now you know we don't believe in curses, Anna. I don't know how you can possibly think that a river can be evil."

Anna looked around fearfully. "I feel it in my bones," she whispered. "It's just something I *know*. That river is going to bring you trouble. Pack up your family, Rebecca!" she urged. "Move up to higher ground. Don't wait..."

Rebecca sighed. "You know what Lorenzo always says – "

"Move to Newburgh? Over my dead body!" chanted Henry with a mischievous smile.

Anna wagged her finger and said, "Well, you can't say you weren't warned." She looked up at the cloudless sky. "I've done all I can to help. I'd best be leaving while the day is looking so pretty. Did you remember that it's the first day of spring?"

Rebecca nodded. "And the Lord remembered, too. Look! He sent us sunshine, squawking blue jays, chirping frogs – even the floodwater is down a bit. It's a perfect day for our mystery guest to wake up."

The women linked arms and walked together to the

edge of the Carter clearing.

"I want you to be the first to know, Anna," Rebecca whispered. "We'll be needing you back here in September to help bring the next Carter into the world." She smiled shyly and patted her tummy.

"Land's sake, you never give up, do you, woman?"

"Lord willing, this will be my last."

The women hugged, and then Anna called back to the cabin where Henry stood with Laura by the door. "Laura, you take care of your mother, now. And mind those poultices. And Henry, you try and stay out of trouble, ya hear?"

Shortly after Anna left, the stranger woke up. The first thing he did was kick the poultices off his feet.

"Mother! Laura! Hurry! The sick man is trying to get up!" shouted Henry. He was obediently watching their guest.

Laura and Polly were helping their mother wash shirts and petticoats in the spring that flowed out of the hill next to their cabin.

"Polly, mind these clothes. Laura, you'd better come with me."

They lifted their skirts and ran to the cabin. Their patient was propped up on one elbow looking at Henry with wild-eyed confusion.

"My father says that you would'a been wolf bait if you didn't get rescued," Henry was saying, "And he should know, because he knows everything about wolves. Bears, too, and I said that maybe the wolves left you alone 'cause the rattlers already..."

"Henry! Hush! Don't bother our guest with your silly stories," Rebecca scolded. "Go out and help Polly with the washing. And mind you don't get the shirts dirtier than they already are."

"Ah, do I have to? That's woman's work. I'd best be..." A glance at his mother's sparking eyes silenced his argument.

"All right," he said, "but I'll be back quicker than a toad can nip a fly, you just wait and see." He ran off to the spring, shouting for Polly to hurry up and start spreading the clothes out for drying.

Rebecca hesitated, but not her spirited daughter. Laura knelt down by the stranger's toes to reset the poultice. Large water-filled blisters had bubbled up all over the top sides of both his feet, but the flesh in his toes was gray and lifeless.

"We'll have to make some new poultices," Laura murmured. "I'll wet these down before I mix up some more." She replaced one of the pungent molds, but the stranger inhaled sharply and kicked it off. She looked helplessly at her mother.

"You have to leave that on," Rebecca explained gently. She gestured for Laura to go and get some broth from the pot warming by the fire. "It'll sting at first, but you'll lose your feet if we can't get the swelling and blisters healed."

Rebecca moved to his feet and patted the poultice back into shape. "This is flaxseed oil mixed with cornmeal and lime water. It'll dry up your wounds, but you can't take it off anymore."

He studied her warily, his mouth twisted in a painful grimace. He was sweating from the strain of sitting up. Finally he relaxed his arm and fell back, closing his eyes and breathing hard from the exertion.

"Maybe he doesn't speak English," whispered Laura when she returned with a steamy bowl of broth.

"Did you see your toes? Are you in pain? Do you remember why you're here?" asked Rebecca in progressively louder tones.

The stranger gulped and tensed, but still ignored them. He seemed to be holding his breath. Henry came running back into the cabin, but stopped at the door.

"Polly didn't need any help," he announced. "I'll bet he's hungry," he added.

"Let me help you with this broth," said Laura, kneeling beside him.

The stranger stayed silent.

Rebecca set a poultice on one foot, and then the other. His jaw clenched and his knees jerked, but this time, he let the damp molds stay. She gestured for Laura to put down the steamy bowl and go outside.

"We're here to help you," said Rebecca softly. "Whenever you're ready to eat, you just go ahead. Laura put a bowl next to you and there's a whole big pot of broth warming by the fire. And don't worry about eating too much. My husband sees to it that we always have plenty."

She gestured for Henry to come in and sit down next

to him again. "I have to go out to make sure Henry hasn't ruined the wash," she said. "He'll be here if you need help, so try to make yourself comfortable. Be sure to leave the poultices on and never mind about wolves and rattlers and ghosts in the woods. Those are just a little boy's stories. It's true that things are bad, but not near as bad as all that."

Rebecca stood up and rubbed her lower back. She sighed and brushed away a tear of exhaustion as Henry settled himself on the floor next to the bowl of broth. He let her smooth his hair and rub his shoulders.

"If it's not one thing, it's always another," she whispered. "Anna Gun's right, son. Life *is* hard here in the Cleveland settlement, and I'm beginning to believe that it will never get any easier. Not ever until the end of time itself."

"Shucks, Mother, that's a long time," said Henry.

"Yes," she said, smiling gently as she reached down to hug her little boy. "That's forever, Henry. But somehow we'll make it through. Carters always have. Somehow, someday, we'll all make it through...."

POWWOW

Master Adams had been too ill to teach school all week, so Polly and Henry kept busy by helping to look after their mysterious guest.

"I have an idea," said Henry. "Let's swap stories with him. We'll tell him things about us, and then he'll tell us things about him."

"What if he doesn't want to?" asked Polly. "What if he can't even hear? Laura thinks he doesn't speak like us, Mother says he's too sad to talk, and you know what Father thinks..."

"Yep. Scared. He's just plain chicken hearted."

"Chicken hearted about what?"

"Us, I guess," said Henry. "Or maybe something really bad happened to him, and he's afraid it's going to happen again. Like that time our new house burned down. Biggest house in the whole Cleveland settlement, the only one with clapboards, all trimmed and fancy like Mother had in Vermont, not even finished, and just like that..."

He snapped his fingers. "....gone. All from a few lousy sparks in the shavings pile. I was mighty afraid of fires after that happened."

Her dark eyes widened. "Me, too," she said solemnly. "I remember. I was four."

Henry and Polly sat cross-legged on the floor next to the lower bunk in the garret that was attached to the side of the Carter cabin. They studied the blanketed man who was either sleeping or pretending to sleep.

"He's getting skinnier," whispered Polly.

Henry nodded. "And weaker."

Ten days had passed since his rescue. During that time, his only utterances had been feverish mumbles. Major Carter said that more privacy would help him regain his strength and dignity, so he and Alonzo pulled him into the garret by using his bedroll as a sledge. Alonzo looked after his chamber pot and Laura left plates of food next to his bed. If she offered to help, he refused to eat. So she simply came back later for the empty dishes.

Poultices were no longer needed on his toes and the blisters covering the top of his feet were almost gone. His toes were still too horrible for Polly's faint heart, but Henry was getting used to them. They seemed to be shriveling up like dried fruit, looking more and more like they had been carved out of charred wood. Polly worried that they were turning into corks.

Suddenly Henry's eyes brightened. He leaped up and screamed, "FIRE! The blankets are on fire! Everybody out!"

The stranger jolted up in bed.

"You see, Polly! He can hear! He understands!"

Polly, who had been completely fooled and was already outside running for the spring, came back wagging her finger.

"You little devil," she said. "You're going to scare Mother half to death."

"Ah, shucks, no one else heard me." Henry and their guest stared at each other. They both smiled.

"It was a good plan, wasn't it, mister?"

He nodded so slightly that the children weren't sure if he had really responded.

"Ask him something else," whispered Polly.

"You hear and understand everything we say, don't you?"

This time his nod was unmistakable.

"Henry, he likes you. I'll get Mother!" Polly ran off to the kitchen to spread the news.

"We don't have much time to talk before they all come crowding in."

He nodded again, but his smile was gone.

"What should we know about you?"

He looked deep into Henry's eyes and cleared his throat. "I ain't chicken hearted." His voice was almost too low and raspy to hear.

Henry leaned closer. "Oh, I knew you wasn't," he said. "Anybody who goes out on Lake Erie in March can't be. What's your name, anyway?"

"Ben."

"Are you hurting much, Ben?"

He nodded and looked away.

"I guess you're not used to lying around all day. My father says you must be part black bear. Big as one and sleepy as one, too. Why are you so sad, mister?"

"My boy."

"Me?"

The stranger's eyes brimmed with tears. He shook his head.

"My boy. He gone, now."

And that was all he'd say. He pulled the quilt up over his massive shoulder and turned toward the wall.

"Don't quit on me, Ben. What's your boy's name? Mister?" Henry was about to touch his shoulder, but he changed his mind and pulled his hand away.

"I'll tell everyone that you've gone back to sleep," whispered Henry. "We'll talk about your boy tomorrow."

The next morning, Henry was so excited that he ate his breakfast while pacing back and forth beside Ben's bed.

"Hey, Ben, wake up. The mush gets hard and lumpy if you don't eat it while it's hot." Henry set a large wooden bowl next to the bed.

"Laura usually brings your food, but today I said I would since I had to come early if I was going to come at all. We're getting ready for the big spring powwow. We're expecting hundreds of Chippewas to show up any day now."

Ben sat up and began to eat.

"You feeling better this morning?"

He nodded.

"Well anyway, at about this time every year, when the

38

maple sugar sap stops running, Chippewa braves come out of the woods and do their trading right here in Cleveland before moving on to their summer camps further west. They come paddling down the Cuyahoga, sometimes so loaded down they have to tow an extra canoe to hold all the furs and jugs of honey and maple sugar they've been collecting all winter. You should see all the piles of furs! And they have bear oil and venison, too. Heaps of it, mostly dried and ready to trade."

"I was hopin' to do some trappin' here in the Cuyahoga Valley myself," said Ben between scoops. His face was less puffy this morning and his eyes were bright and lively. He seemed almost happy to have Henry's company.

"And talk about dancing and whooping and whiskey drinking! They give all their rifles and tomahawks to the women, build a huge fire, and then have the biggest celebration you ever saw! Old Bryant's still will be dry tonight!"

"They got good whiskey here?"

Henry shrugged. "I don't rightly know myself, but the drifters and trappers who hang around and do odd chores for my father seem to like it just fine. A few years ago, David and Gilman Bryant brought a still up here from Virginia – is that where you're from, Ben?"

He shook his head. "Kentucky. But we was comin' here from the Michigan Territory."

"That don't make no sense. Michigan is north, Kentucky is south...."

"Me and my boy, Willie, we left Kentucky last fall. We worked our way through Indiana and spent the winter near Fort Detroit helpin' to rebuild after their bad fire last year. But then there was no more work in Michigan. Cold, too."

"So you decided to come to Cleveland?"

He nodded.

"Just you and Willie?"

"No, they was five of us in one canoe."

"Five? Three besides you and Willie?"

He nodded. "They was my boss, Massa' Hunter, an' his woman, an' their child. He need me to row him over, an' we was all goin' to settle west a' here."

"What happened?"

"Bad storm."

"Oh, we had that storm, too. Lots of hail and thunder. It caused a landslide that ruined the best joke I ever thought of."

Ben set his empty bowl on the floor and stared wide-eyed out the door. "Our trip from Detroit be goin' good. The wind push on our backs the whole way. But on our third day out when we look for a spot to camp, we couldn't find no place to suit Massa' Hunter. Then a bad wind come outta' no where. The waves be so big, they about swallow the canoe. Then the ice start to fall. We go for land, but the canoe.... "

"Tipped, didn't it?"

Ben nodded and lowered his head, covering his eyes with one of his huge calloused hands. Henry sat on the floor next to the bowl and leaned his elbows on the bed.

41

"My father says that there's been plenty of wrecks by the Rocky River. It's those steep cliffs over there. No decent place to land. Did you climb the rocks to get up out of the water?"

He nodded solemnly and sat quietly for a few seconds.

"My boy, my Willy, he try to swim, same as me. But he go down under a big wave. It come and wash over me and him. It push us under and kinda' grab our legs. Willie stay down, same as the Hunter child."

"Couldn't you grab his hand?"

Ben hung his head. "It be too dark to see. An' the ice be beatin' down on us. An' the cold water, it about freeze my legs stiff. Me and Massa' Hunter, we try to go back for our boys, but the storm, it pull them further and further away."

Henry's stomach tightened.

"My Willie be ten years old. Like you."

Henry knew it wasn't the right time to tell him that he wouldn't be ten until December thirteenth, but he couldn't think of anything else to say. So he just sat there feeling sick and sorry, hoping that Ben wouldn't mind his silence.

"Willie be home, now."

"Home?"

Ben's eyes, large and sad, locked onto Henry's. "He be in heaven, now, with the Lord."

"Is he an angel?"

"I believe so. Willie be watchin' and waitin' for his daddy to come along an' join him one day. I been layin' here thinkin' that he just fine up there and that I got to go on without him for a while."

"What happened to the others?"

"Massa' Hunter's woman, she swim to shore, but she pass on the next day," said Ben softly. "She be so cold, she just close her eyes an' go to sleep. It be too wet for fire, and the rain, it mix with snow, and it keep comin' more an' more. Next night, the wolves come."

"Wolves? A pack of big gray ones?"

Ben shrugged. "Mighta' been gray. It be so dark, it hard to see."

"How did you get away?"

"I be asleep in a lil' cave outta' the wind. Massa' Hunter, he won't leave his woman alone by the water. He be cold, an' talkin' crazy-like. Then he start yellin' but when I go over, I hear runnin' and snarlin' in the bushes. An' I hear howlin'. *Bad* howlin'. Next day, they was both gone."

"The wolves have been starving this winter," said Henry. "My father says that every family in the Cuyahoga Valley has lost sheep and hogs."

Ben sighed and shook his head. "It weren't supposed to be like this. Willy an' me, we left Kentucky so we could have a new life. The Cuyahoga River an' the Ohio lands was goin' to give us a chance to do things our way. Not like this." He pointed to his mangled feet.

Henry was trying to understand how Ben could have survived. "You wrecked in the storm Thursday night," he said. "And Mrs. Hunter died on Friday, the wolves came on Saturday, but the trappers didn't find you until Monday. Did you have food with you?"

"A piece a' dried meat in my pocket. The supplies an' the boat, they all break up an' wash away in the storm. I drank the lake an' kept prayin' an' lookin' for my Willie, tryin' to get warm. The wolves, they come back at night, so I climb the tree over the water, an' that's where them trappers find me."

After a long pause, Ben lifted his head and took a deep breath. "It's time I get up. I be layin' here long enough."

"You think you can walk by yourself?"

He looked determined. "I gots to do it some time."

Henry pointed to the corner. "Alonzo made you some walking sticks. I'll get them."

Ben tossed away the quilt and pulled his homespun night shirt over his knees. With a deep breath, he swung his legs off the bed. But when his feet touched the floor, he fell back with a horrible groan.

Henry almost cried at the sight of his contorted face. "Father! Alonzo! Help!"

Having just finished breakfast, they were walking out to the barn when they heard Henry's cries. They ran in and immediately understood the problem. They gently pulled Ben up, and together, one on each side, helped him stand.

"Try putting your weight on your heels," said the Major. "You'll split that new skin if you put too much pressure on the front of your feet. There – easy.... "

Ben managed to balance on his heels, but then his legs began to quiver and shake. He fell back and covered his face in shame.

"It ain't no use, Massa'. I done lost my legs."

"You've just got to build them up, is all," said the Major. "They've gotten all puny these last two weeks. And anyway," he added, "I'm no master."

"Yes, sir."

"Most folks call me Major Carter. Or just plain Lorenzo suits me fine. We don't take to that Virginia master talk around here. My Rebecca says that there's just one master in this world and it's like taking His name in vain to use that word for anyone else. She won't stand for it. And I won't stand for anything she won't stand for... "

"Yes, sir."

"My son tells me that you're called Ben, is that right?"

"Yes, sir."

"You should know, here in Cleveland, we don't take to trading men. We have enough troubles trading furs and whiskey."

"Yes, sir."

"Now, you're going to have to stop that."

"Stop what, sir?"

"All that sir talk. That may have been the thing to do where you came from, but around here, children are the only ones who do it. Men don't. A man has to be his own boss in order to survive in the Cuyahoga wilderness."

Ben nodded. "Yes, sir." He glanced at the Major and smiled shyly.

"It might take a while, sir – ah, Major..."

The Major's eyes softened. "Are you sure you're ready to get up today?"

"I gots to try."

"It's as warm as summer this morning," said Alonzo. "And we could use some help watching for the Chippewa braves to come paddling around the bend. The river is so crooked you'll be able to see them a long time before they finally reach the landing."

"Ben can do that," said Henry. "Right? You can watch the river for us, can't you? Even if it don't make no sense how a river could ever be so crooked as the Cuyahoga?"

"It be the least I can do, the way I been layin' here day after day," he mumbled.

"Do you have enough backbone to lift him?" the Major asked his oldest son.

"I won't know until I try," said Alonzo, flexing his muscles.

"No, sir – uh – no, Major, I mean – it be best that I do this myself."

The two men looked into each other's eyes and Major Carter nodded his understanding. "All right, then," he said gruffly. "Come on, boys. We've got work to do in the barn."

As they walked away with the milking pails, Henry glanced back to see Ben's head and shoulders appear around the cabin door, with the rest of him following close behind. He crawled on his hands and knees to the hill overlooking the Cuyahoga River and kept a faithful watch for the rest of the day, just as he said he would.

5

ECLIPSE

"Where's Doans Corners?" asked Ben as he hobbled along after Henry and Alonzo toward the river. It was June 17 and they were waiting for Major Carter to return from a muster of a local regiment of the Ohio State Militia.

"Oh, about four miles east of here," said Alonzo. "The militia trained yesterday and celebrated all night, so Father should be along any time. He said that it was a bad time to be away, but as an officer, it was his duty to be there."

"We're not supposed to leave the tavern unguarded," said Henry.

"Why not?" asked Ben.

"Master Adams said that there's supposed to be a solar eclipse today," Henry said. "But I think he's joshin'. It's just plain impossible for the moon, that's smaller than the earth, to block the sun, that's a lot bigger than the earth. It don't make sense..."

"We'll have to see for ourselves," said Alonzo.

"What's all that got to do with standin' guard?" asked Ben, looking worried.

"Father was afraid that the eclipse might cause trouble between the Seneca and Chippewa tribes," said Alonzo.

"What kinda' trouble?" asked Ben.

Alonzo shrugged. "Panic. Or maybe fighting. Who knows? They might blame each other for the eclipse, thinking it was a curse or something. Father is about the only one around here who can settle problems between them without a whole lot of bloodshed."

"Like that time a couple years ago when he stopped a war right here at the Cuyahoga?" asked Henry, his eyes shining with pride.

Alonzo nodded and then explained to Ben. "The brother of Stigwanish, the Seneca chief, stabbed and killed a Chippewa medicine man because his wife died after being treated by him. So to get even, the Chippewas painted their faces black and lined up on the west side of the river, ready to attack the Senecas on the east side. Our cabin was the only thing between them."

"They paint their faces black?" asked Ben with a big grin.

"Yeah, I guess you'd be a natural Chippewa," joked Alonzo. "But only for battles."

"No wonder they look at me kinda' funny. How'd the Major stop the fight?"

"He offered the Chippewas a whole gallon of whiskey if they'd take the body of the medicine man west to the Rocky River for burial," said Alonzo. "They agreed, but Bryant couldn't get the whiskey made in time. So Father offered them an extra gallon if they'd wait peacefully.

48

Finally, Bryant came through with the firewater, and they left as promised. Father didn't sleep for two whole nights."

"So the moon's supposed to block the sun in the middle of the day?" asked Ben doubtfully.

"And it's supposed to get dark?" asked Henry.

Alonzo nodded. "And we want to be out on Lake Erie to see it. There's not a cloud in the sky, so if we paddle our canoe far enough from shore, the trees won't block our view. Then afterward, we'll go and check if the juniper berries are ripe at an old Indian mound just east of here. Bryant has offered to buy the berries. He wants to make gin."

"That ain't what your mama say," said Ben.

"That's right," said Henry. "She said that she wants the berries to season the deer meat."

"Well, it sounds like we might have a war after all," laughed Alonzo. "The war of the juniper berries. Who do you think would win? Bryant or the mother of the great woodsman, Alonzo Carter?"

"Probably the mother of the even greater woodsman, *Henry* Carter," said Henry.

"Uh oh, we don't want no fightin'. We best pick two baskets," said Ben, laughing along.

During his three months in Cleveland, Ben had recovered his strength, but not his toes. The three smallest on each foot had completely shriveled and broken off. Despite problems with balancing, swollen joints, and aching muscles, he quietly helped with chores in the Carter cabin and vegetable garden. He never talked about himself during their frequent fishing trips on Lake Erie and up the Cuyahoga River, but as he paddled the Carter canoe, he taught Henry and Alonzo several spirituals and work songs that always made the going easier.

Barking dogs heralded the arrival of Major Carter back at the tavern, so Alonzo loaded berry baskets, fishing poles, and his prized rifle into the canoe. The gun had been a gift from his father on his sixteenth birthday.

"We're leaving!" he shouted up toward the hill.

Major Carter appeared, waving his rifle in a farewell gesture.

"Don't be out too long!" shouted the Major. "And watch that you're not blinded by the eclipse!"

Alonzo nodded and waved as he pushed the canoe out into the river. The Cuyahoga was only a foot deep now that the spring rains had been replaced by unusually dry weather.

"Blinded?" asked Ben. "What the Major mean by that?"

Alonzo shrugged as though it didn't really matter. "Master Adams has been warning everyone not to look straight at the sun during the eclipse. He said that men back East have burned their eyes that way. You ever seen an eclipse, Ben?"

He shook his head. "An' I won't believe it till I see it."

"Me neither," said Henry.

As they approached Lake Erie, it began to get darker and noticeably colder. With no wind, the water was almost mirror-like when they glided out onto the lake. They paddled away from the forested shoreline and looked up at the strange sight of the moon partially covering the sun. The sky was still as blue as ever, but the moon appeared to be dark purple as it moved slowly in front of the sun.

"It *is* bright," said Alonzo, squinting and rubbing his eyes. "I'm going to shield my eyes, just in case Master Adams is right."

Ben rested his paddle across his lap and shaded his eyes with his massive hands. No birds cried. No fish jumped. No branches snapped. All of nature seemed to be waiting and watching as the sun's light gradually faded. Henry shivered.

"It true," whispered Ben. "The sun be gone. Oh, I wish my Willy be here to see this!"

"It's like night!" gasped Henry.

And then, just as the blackened moon was in the very center of the sun and completely surrounded by a narrow ring of harsh yellow light, a shrill wail rose up out of the woods.

"Demons!" hissed Ben. "Oh Lord, carry me home. Carry me home!"

"Mrs. Gun is right!" whispered Henry. "It's evil spirits, on the rampage!"

The howling grew louder and more intense, but it wasn't until one of the plaintive cries ended in a whoop that Alonzo realized that the ghostly wails were being made by distraught Senecas, most likely reacting to the unexpected midday darkness. They often camped on the east side of the River.

"Evil spirits, my eye," scoffed Alonzo. "It's the Indians, you chicken hearted fool. Most likely they didn't know the eclipse was coming."

Ben stopped praying but he and Henry nervously watched the shoreline for signs of movement.

"Master Adams says that the moon will block the sun for a minute or two, then it will start to get light again," Alonzo said. "Look! The moon has already moved closer to the other side. It'll be over pretty soon."

As the bright light of midday gradually returned, the mournful cries faded away. Finally, a lone raven screeched, *All's well! All's well!* Its announcement seemed to signal a return to nature's normal stirrings. As if startled awake from a midday nap, a flock of white gulls suddenly fluttered off the sand. Then a dog began to bark from somewhere deep in the woods.

"Do you see that hill over there?" asked Alonzo, pointing to shore. "That's the old Indian mound where the Juniper trees are. We can pull the canoe up on the sand just below it."

Ben nodded and turned toward shore. "What's in the mound?" he asked.

"No one knows for sure. I've found old arrow heads and pieces of pottery there, but I've never dug down in it. It's probably just a big old heap of bones. Stigwanish told my father that a completely different tribe of Indians lived here a long time ago. There's mounds and old forts all the way up and down the Cuyahoga. He says there's a giant mound shaped like a serpent in Southern Ohio."

"A rattler?" asked Henry.

"I don't know. Ask him the next time you see him," said Alonzo.

"What happened to those Indians?" asked Ben.

Alonzo shrugged. "If the river used to be anything like it is now, they were probably flooded out or chased away by sickness or enemies."

"The curse of the Cuyahoga musta' got them," Ben said softly.

"Now where'd you hear that?" asked Alonzo.

"From Henry, mostly. An' Miz Gun."

"Henreeee..." accused Alonzo. "You shouldn't be telling stories about a Cuyahoga curse. You know Father doesn't allow any talk that might stop settlers from coming here, especially talk about superstitious nonsense like that."

"Mrs. Gun talks like that all the time," said Henry.

"Well, you're not Mrs. Gun."

"Oh, really?" smirked Henry.

Alonzo sneered at him as they beached the canoe. "I'll beat you to the top," said Henry as he swung his legs out. He pushed aside thorny shrubs to scamper up the sandy embankment, turning just in time to catch the baskets that Alonzo heaved after him.

Ben used his canoe paddle like a crutch, and Alonzo pulled himself up by hanging onto bare roots. On the other side of the ancient mound, a cluster of Juniper trees stretched out their prickly boughs. Ben held the branches down while Alonzo and Henry picked the dark blue berries. Then they sat down to enjoy the wild strawberries they found in the long grass on the edge of the embankment.

"Do you hear drumbeats?" asked Alonzo.

Ben nodded, but his eyes grew as big as saucers. "An' somethin' else," he whispered. In a sunny spot about six feet behind Alonzo, a coiled rattlesnake sat poised to strike, its head erect and its rattles humming with increasing intensity. Ben shoved Alonzo roughly out of the way just as it sprang forward. He used the broad end of his paddle to block the snake's bite. It thudded against the wood, then whipped around to slither away into the underbrush.

"Hey, what's the big idea?" complained Alonzo, rubbing his bruised shoulder.

Henry caught the motion of the retreating snake out of the corner of his eye. "Whoa, that's a big one!" he said.

"A big what?" asked Alonzo, still irritated.

"A big rattler! Ben saved your life!"

Ben winked at Henry. "What? You call that big? Weren't nothin' but a worm."

"A worm with fangs aimed right at Alonzo," said Henry.

"I guess it don't like the taste a' wood," laughed Ben. "Didn't stay around for a second helpin'."

Alonzo turned to look, but the snake was gone. "This sure is turning out to be *some* day," he said, shaking his head, his heart suddenly racing as he realized how close he had come to being bitten. "Our first eclipse, and now this

– thanks, Ben. I can't think of anything worse than a rattler bite. You saved me and I owe you a lot, now."

"You owe me nothin'," he said gruffly. "You Carters been savin' me everyday. I ain't never gonna' live long enough to ever pay ya'll back."

"There's no reason to pay – "

"Yes, there is. I always pay what I owe."

"And so do I," countered Alonzo. "And I say I owe you for stopping that rattler attack. I'd be feeling mighty poorly right now if it wasn't for you. So I owe *you,* and that's that!"

Embarrassed, they stared quietly out at Lake Erie and finished the last of their strawberries. "Let's see what's happening with those drumbeats," Alonzo said, eager to change the subject.

He picked through the thick bushes, carefully searching and listening for more rattlesnakes. As they crept away from the shoreline, the smooth undulations of Seneca singing, accented by sporadic claps and high pitched whelps, grew louder. Smelling tobacco smoke, Alonzo signaled Ben and Henry to stay back. He peeked through an opening in the leaves and saw a small band of Seneca braves, their squaws, and a few little children gathered around a great bonfire.

The popular and familiar Seneca chief, Stigwanish, was seated in a place of honor. Younger braves, some wearing wooden faces, others in masks made from braided corn husks, sang and danced to a steady drum beat. They took long drinks from a jug that was being passed around.

A white dog, apparently strangled, hung limply from an elevated platform near the fire.

Alonzo held a finger to his lips and gestured for Ben and Henry to come forward. The singing and chanting was occasionally interrupted by emotional speeches delivered with excited, wide-armed gestures toward the sky. After watching several minutes, Alonzo nodded for them to go back toward their canoe.

"My father speaks both Algonquin and the Iroquois language," Alonzo told Ben when they were out of hearing range. "But I only know a few words, not enough to understand what they were saying."

"What they be doin' with that dead dog?"

"From what Gilman Bryant says, they sacrifice it to their most powerful god, the Great Manitou. They believe that the dog's soul delivers their thanks for their blessings and also, their prayers for good luck."

"How he know?"

"He went to a White Dog Feast a couple years ago," said Alonzo. "And he speaks Iroquois real good. But I thought he said that a white dog is only sacrificed in February, to bring good luck for the new year."

Henry smirked. "You thought wrong, Alonzo. It ain't February now."

"They must be having a special ceremony because of the eclipse."

"We best be gettin' outta' here," interrupted Ben, nervous about being discovered. He studied the place where the rattlesnake had disappeared.

"Oh, I don't think we need to worry about being bothered by the Senecas," said Alonzo. "Stigwanish was there. He's been a good friend to the Cleveland settlers, especially to Father."

"No, Alonzo," argued Henry. "They might be upset

about the eclipse. And I know they wouldn't like us snooping at their singing and dancing. We wasn't invited. You know how Father always warns us to stay away from their ceremonies...."

"Yes, sir. We best leave *now*," urged Ben.

Goose bumps suddenly puckered Alonzo's bare arm as he remembered that it was Stigwanish's brother who had committed Cleveland's first murder. Would one brother follow in the same footsteps as the other? He shuddered.

"You're right, Ben. Let's get out of here!" he said.

Alonzo picked up the baskets of juniper berries and scurried down the steep embankment. Ben followed by sliding down feet first, while Henry threw the canoe paddle over the edge and jumped down after it. They hurried into the canoe and pushed off, silently gliding away over the clear blue lake.

With a tremendous sigh of relief, Ben dipped his paddle into the water and began to hum one of his favorite rowing songs.

Alonzo grinned. "Well, if the Senecas can sing, so can we!" The boys joined in, singing and paddling together in a steady rhythm as they skimmed across the water.

> *Swing low, sweet chariot,*
> *Comin' for to carry me home.*
> *Swing low, sweet chariot,*
> *Comin' for to carry me home...*

6

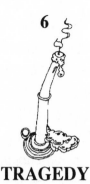

TRAGEDY

July and August were hotter and drier than usual, but there was just enough rain to keep the swamp on the west side of the Cuyahoga moist and filled with rotting plants and animals. The warm temperatures produced foul vapors so thick with mosquitoes that every living being was imprisoned in buzzing, stinging clouds of pure misery. And as though Clevelanders hadn't suffered quite enough, the dreaded ague struck with merciless tyranny during the first week of September.

Thankfully, in the Carter household, only Ben, Henry, and Polly were sick this year. Major Carter never admitted to having chills and fevers, and Alonzo and Laura had been so ill in previous years, that their bodies were finally accustomed to fighting the disease. Rebecca never seemed to get as sick when she was expecting a baby, and mysteriously, two-year-old Mercy was totally unaffected.

Poor Henry was so weak that he could hardly get out of bed to use the privy behind the cabin. His attacks of bone rattling chills and sheet soaking fevers came twice each day, once as the sun rose in the morning, and again, as it sank away into the western woods. He'd had only mild cases in the past and had been able to get his chores done between shaking fits, but this year, he didn't even have the strength to eat.

Ben also suffered ague spells twice each day, but he stubbornly tried to ignore the disease as he took over Henry's milking and wood chopping chores. He was a great help in the vegetable garden, too, especially since Rebecca's pregnancy had progressed to the point where she was unable to do much besides supervise the meals and look after Henry. Polly's attacks were less predictable, coming only every other day or so. A long nap was usually all she needed to restore her strength.

"You've got to at least *try* to get out of bed, Henry," said Major Carter one muggy morning in early September. "We're picking corn today. It looks like we might have a bumper crop. I'm helping the girls, so Alonzo and Ben need you on their team. Don't you want to help?"

Henry opened his eyes and nodded.

"You'll feel better outside in the fresh air. The cabin's so hot that it makes your fever seem worse than it really is."

Henry propped himself up and accepted a steamy cup of his mother's bark tea. His thin arms trembled as he forced himself to drink it.

"Do you want Alonzo to carry you across the river? I'll send him for you later this morning," his father offered, somewhat more sympathetically.

Henry shook his head and squeezed his eyes shut as he

swallowed the bitter tea. "No. I'll wait for these chills to stop, and then I'll wade across the sandbar. The water will feel good."

Major Carter nodded and ruffled his son's grimy hair. "You could use a bath, too."

Henry forced a trembling smile.

"Show the ague who's boss, son. Before you know it, you'll feel good as new."

Henry nodded, but couldn't stop the convulsive shivering that suddenly wracked his wasted body. He clenched his jaw so that his teeth wouldn't chatter in front of his father.

Major Carter looked away, but then impulsively, turned back to lift Henry into his arms as he knelt beside the bed.

"There now," he said softly. "I'll warm you, Henry. You've got to put some meat on those bones and fight this thing, son. It won't last much longer if you eat and get out of bed. No one ever gets better just lying around."

He cradled his son until the shaking subsided, then gently laid Henry back on the lumpy corn husk mattress. Weak and exhausted, tears silently streamed down the sunken shadows beneath the boy's eyes and dripped onto his fever soaked sheets.

"I'll get up today, I promise," Henry whispered as his father rose to leave. "I won't be chicken hearted no more, you'll see..."

The whole Carter family, except for Rebecca and Henry, worked to harvest the corn. They would eventually use every part of it. The husks were always needed to replenish the tavern mattresses, the cobs made good kindling in the winter, and the stalks and leaves were dried for animal fodder. Some was eaten like a vegetable, but most of the kernels would be dried and scraped off the cobs, then ground for meal.

When they first came to Cleveland, they had to pound the corn themselves with a clumsy handmill. But now that there was a water powered gristmill in Newburgh, corn production had greatly increased and most families had plenty for their own uses. Leftover corn was sold to the Bryants to distill into whiskey. Without reliable and regular transportation to the East, there was no other market.

Little Mercy raced between the mounds of corn and hopped over tree stumps that would eventually be removed during the less hectic winter months. "Mercy pick corn! Mercy pick corn!" she sang as she dropped her two ears into a large basket at the edge of the field.

Ben and Alonzo, both laden with sturdy bags already bulging with corn, laughed at her antics. They had begun harvesting near the river, while Laura, Polly, and the Major started on the far west side. They were competing to see which team could pick the most.

"Make sure you put your corn in our basket, Mercy," shouted Alonzo.

"No! Mercy help Laura and Polly," she said with a teasing grin.

"Oh no you don't!" said Alonzo, pretending to rush at her with tickling fingers. "Join our team, Mercy! Without

Henry, we need a third helper, and anyway, we're going to have the most by the end of the day!"

She ran back toward her sisters, squealing her favorite word, "Noooooo!"

As Alonzo emptied his bag, he saw Henry trip on a root in the path on the other side of the river, just below their cabin.

"Hey!" he called back into the field. "Look who's up and around!"

Ben swiped a hand across his forehead and squinted in the bright sun. "Henry be feelin' better," he said. "He finally outta' bed."

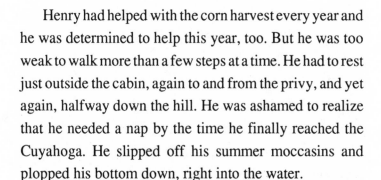

Henry had helped with the corn harvest every year and he was determined to help this year, too. But he was too weak to walk more than a few steps at a time. He had to rest just outside the cabin, again to and from the privy, and yet again, halfway down the hill. He was ashamed to realize that he needed a nap by the time he finally reached the Cuyahoga. He slipped off his summer moccasins and plopped his bottom down, right into the water.

Henry hoped that the river would smother the fever that seemed to burn away all his strength. If this day was like the others, his next shaking fit would not strike until dusk, so he had the whole afternoon to somehow find the *real* Henry and get rid of the puny stranger that had taken over his body and spirit. If he could just cool off, he'd he able to pick mountains of corn and show everyone that he wasn't a weakling after all. But he was so tired. Perhaps if he just closed his eyes for a minute or two....

Henry slid further into the soothing Cuyahoga, laying his head back, wetting his hair, immersing his ears, so that all he could hear was the rapid rushing of his own blood as it pulsed through his achy head.

Pah-pum. Pah-pum. Pah-pum.

Only his face showed as the cool and silky water flowed over him, washing away the sweat, washing away the pain. It was good to be clean again. Henry felt more like his old self, but he was so tired, more tired than he had ever been. With the sun so bright, the reflections so shiny, he closed his eyes and relaxed, lulled into a deep and restful sleep.

Pah-pum. Pah-pum. Pah-pum.

---◇---

Across the river, Alonzo emptied his corn bag again. He realized that Henry had still not joined them. *I'd better go and carry him over the sandbar,* he thought. He glanced at the landing. *Where's Henry? Did he go back up the hill?*

Alonzo squinted in the bright midday sun. He shielded his eyes and focused on the eastern shoreline, then slowly scanned the glittering Cuyahoga, up and down, back and forth. The sunny reflections contrasted sharply with the black shadows along the river banks, making it impossible to see what was actually there. *Was that Henry under the water? Was that a hand or something else bobbing in the river?*

Alonzo shouted, "Henry!"

Ben limped over, dragging his full bag behind him. "What be wrong?" he asked.

"I don't see Henry. Is that him under the water over there?"

Ben looked where Alonzo pointed. "I don't know. We best go see."

Alonzo rushed down the western bank below the corn field.

"Henry!"

He ran through the shallow water, darting between the east and west sides, back and forth, splashing, tripping, gasping. Each step stirred up the muddy river bottom, turning the water into a cloudy, murky mess.

"I can't even see my feet anymore! Is he back at the cabin?" he shouted to Ben, who was already hobbling across to the landing. Ben moaned with deep anguish when he saw Henry's moccasins on the river bank.

"Henry!" he bellowed. "Henry!"

Hearing their cries, Rebecca appeared at the top of the path, flushed and breathing heavily. She cradled her arms beneath her baby-filled belly and squinted down at them.

"He's in the corn field!" she shouted.

"No, ma'am! He be up there?" asked Ben.

Her mouth twisted with sudden fear. "Oh my God! I put my feet up for just a minute. He said he was feeling better. Are you sure he's not in the corn field? You know how he loves to play. He might be hiding behind one of the mounds."

"No, ma'am. He's not in the corn."

"Maybe he's in the privy... or the barn... I'll look for him. Henry! HENRY!"

But he wasn't hiding in the corn field, he wasn't resting along the river bank, he wasn't in the barn or the privy behind the cabin, and he never came back to claim his moccasins. He never came back at all.

Alonzo and the Major combed the Cuyahoga River and Lake Erie shoreline for days. Ben crawled up and down the river banks from morning until night, calling and crying, haunted by the pain of his own son's drowning. Neighbors from Newburgh and Doans Corners canvassed the surrounding forests. They helped Laura take care of her mother and harvested the rest of the Carters' corn.

Polly tried not to cry as she kept Mercy out of the way while hunting dogs prowled through the fields. She hid her tears in the barn when Stigwanish and his finest braves came back empty-handed after sifting through the wide and marshy river mouth. She sobbed into her fist every night, trying to be brave, trying to have hope, but managing only to muffle her fear and sadness.

Everyone searched.

Everyone prayed.

Everyone told Polly to hush.

But after a week, they all finally accepted that Henry was gone. Most believed that he had drowned, that his body had been swept far out into Lake Erie and carried away in the strong and unpredictable undercurrents. Rebecca was heart broken that her youngest son would not have a decent burial, like the others had had....

"At least my Henry's not alone," mourned Rebecca from her bed, unable to get up after he had disappeared.

"He's with the others, now, and we'll all be joining him one of these days," she whispered, clinging to Laura and Polly, who stayed and held her hands for as long as she was awake.

"One of these days, all my babies will be together again," she said, over and over. "One of these days..."

Even though cooler nights had come at last, September was a sad and dreary month for the Carters and all the residents of Cleveland. Only a few days after they had given up searching for Henry, Alonzo was sent dashing up to the ridge to fetch Anna Gun. Despite the sorrows and frustrations, it was time for the newest Carter baby to be born.

Little Betsey, wrinkled and red, overflowing with spirit and as feisty as a baby could be, waved her fists and shrieked her first piercing cries.

Not for Henry.

Not for the other lost babies.

Not for those still sick and suffering.

New little Betsey cried only for life itself, and so did all those who heard her.

7

SLAVERS

A month later, Alonzo and his friend, Adolphus Spafford, were returning from the Kingsbury farm in Newburgh when two horsemen raced by toward Cleveland. They had been invited to pick apples in the Kingsbury orchard, a treat that was well worth the five mile hike. This was the first October that there was enough fruit to share, so they both filled their bags and drooled all the way home as they bragged about their mothers' apple pies.

"Aren't those the men who passed us a while back?" asked Alonzo when they approached the Spafford cabin. "Over there, talking to your father?"

"It looks like the same pair. Listen!" said Adolphus. "It sounds like there's going to be trouble."

"I wouldn't go barging in there, if I were you," shouted Amos Spafford from his cabin door, his rifle resting against his shoulder. He was pointing toward Carter's Tavern, just down the road.

"The Major doesn't take kindly to strangers riding in here and making demands."

The two grim faced men reined in their horses as the

sixteen-year-olds dropped their apples and joined Amos by the cabin. "That's where Ben is hiding, you say?" asked the tall thin one on the gray horse. His face was deeply wrinkled, but his eyes glared with fierce intensity.

"I wouldn't exactly say he's hiding," said Amos.

"What do you mean? Is he working for the tavern keeper?" asked the other man on the black horse. Short and plump, his fleshy red cheeks seemed stuffed like a chipmunk. Both men looked as though they had been on the trail for a long time. Their beards were shaggy and their clothes, although expensive and tailor made, reeked of sweat and grease.

"I wouldn't exactly say he's working, either." Amos glanced at Alonzo, raised his eyebrows, and shrugged.

The strangers looked at each other suspiciously. "Well, what *exactly* would you say?" asked the rider on the gray horse. His thin lips twisted with impatience.

Alonzo examined the strangers carefully. He noted the fine leather craftsmanship of their boots and saddles. These were no ordinary trappers, he decided. But he instinctively disliked them, and apparently, Amos Spafford felt the same way.

"I would exactly say nothin', that's what," answered the elder Spafford. He adjusted his rifle.

"Now see here," continued the scowling one, "you folks are harboring a fugitive slave and we aim to claim him."

"Fugitive slave? Ben's a runaway?" asked Amos, throwing Alonzo a puzzled look.

Alonzo understood why his neighbor was surprised. The Carters had been suspicious about Ben's past, but Alonzo had heard his father say several times that Ben's life was nobody's business but his own. Ben apparently preferred it that way because he never talked about himself. With the Major banning the subject, neither did anyone else.

"Why of course he's a runaway. And we've got the papers right here to prove it," he snarled, patting his saddle bag. His leathery fingers rubbed the long horse pistol holstered next to him.

"Who has papers?" asked Alonzo, stepping forward.

"We do, I told you," he snapped.

"And who might you be?"

"Is this boy with you?" he asked Amos.

"You might say that," he said.

"Well, in that case, I'm Phillip Wallace and this is my brother-in-law, George Cooper," he gestured to his chubby partner on the black horse. "Where we come from, whipper-snappers know how to keep their mouths shut. Apparently you haven't learned that lesson, yet," he sneered.

Alonzo crossed his arms and glared into the steely eyes of the wrinkled horseman. But he held his tongue, remembering what his father always said. *Show an opponent a temper only if you know you can whip him. Otherwise, show him nothing and wait for him to show you how he can be whipped.*

Alonzo took a deep breath and waited, but Amos Spafford couldn't mask his merriment. He snorted and smiled. "Well, Mr. Wallace and Mr. Cooper, this should be *real* interesting. You must think that Ben is a mighty valuable worker, big as he is. You must want him pretty badly, traveling all the way up here to hunt him down."

"He's the best field hand I ever had," muttered Wallace.

"Where'd you two say you came from?" Amos asked, his eyes twinkling.

"We farm a few acres south of the Ohio River, near Lexington, Kentucky," said Cooper from his black horse. "It ain't a big place, but it's enough for both our families."

"You don't say," said Amos. "So you two have been riding all the way from Kentucky? What is that, about 350 miles?"

"At least," he said. "And my backside remembers every one of them."

"You rode the old Indian trails all the way through Ohio?"

They both nodded wearily.

"Anything worth mentioning happen in Cincinnati lately?"

They looked at each other and shook their heads.

"How'd you know to look for Ben here?"

"We posted notices in newspapers in Louisville and Pittsburgh," explained Cooper, "and then we sent hand-bills to all the public houses on the post riders' routes. Finally a couple French trappers claimed they left a big black man off here in March."

"They want the reward," added Wallace, "but we're not paying anything unless we can put him back to work."

"Back to work, you say?" said Amos, grinning at Alonzo. "Did those Frenchies say anything about what kind of health Ben was in the last time they saw him?"

The slave hunters exchanged glances again. "Health? They described him good enough, right down to the jagged scar across his back," said Cooper, his round cheeks turning even redder than before.

"They said he was the biggest, strongest, blackest man they ever saw. That's our Ben," bragged Wallace, his hard eyes narrowing. "We've heard the air is bad around here. Are you trying to tell us there's something wrong with his health?"

"Oh, no, I was just being conversational," said Amos, coughing into his hand to hide a chuckle.

"Is there a boy with him?" asked Cooper.

"Boy? Do you mean a colored boy?" he asked.

"Of course. What other kind of boy would be with a fugitive slave?"

Amos stepped next to Alonzo, winked, and threw his arm around his shoulder. "You know Ben, don't you?"

"You might say that..."

"Have you ever seen him with a boy?"

Alonzo pictured Henry and smiled. "I saw him with a boy whose hair was black as coal."

"Yes, that might be the youngun' we're looking for," said Cooper hopefully. "Was the boy's skin same as his hair?"

Alonzo shrugged. "Well, now that you mention it, the boy I saw him with had skin just like mine. Is that the color you're looking for?"

"Don't fool with us," threatened Wallace.

Alonzo looked smug while Amos turned toward Adolphus at the cabin door. "You ever see a colored boy around here?"

"No, Paw, never."

"I guess that's your answer, then," said Amos to the Kentucky horsemen. "And I wouldn't be neighborly if I didn't warn you once more," he said, giving Alonzo's shoulder a secret squeeze. "You'd best take it slow and easy over at the tavern. Major Carter has been worse tempered than usual. Ain't that right, Alonzo?"

"I'd rather visit an injured bear," he said truthfully.

Both riders snorted. "If he's got our property, there's nothing that's going to stop us from getting it back," muttered the irritated Wallace.

"Nothing?" laughed Amos.

"That's right. You heard me. No one ever gets in our way."

"Well now, this should be the most entertaining thing that's happened this year," Amos said, nodding to Adolphus. "I think we'll walk along and introduce you to the Major ourselves."

"That won't be necessary," snarled Wallace. He wiped a grimy sleeve across his nose, cleared his throat, and spit a slimy blob toward Alonzo. It splattered on his leg as the Kentuckians spurred their horses and trotted away.

"They'll be sorry," said Alonzo as he picked up his bag of apples. He ran through a shortcut in the woods, arriving home just in time to hear his father's outburst.

"Get off my property!" His shout was closely followed by gunfire. "Slavers aren't welcome here!"

"We have papers," protested Wallace. "If you keep Ben, you're violating the Fugitive Slave Law of 1793."

"You ever hear of Carter's law?" sputtered the Major, his dark eyes sparking dangerously. "That's the only law we have around here. Now get going, back to the hole you crawled out of, and don't ever let me see your dirty slave trading faces again!"

The Kentucky farmers pulled back and looked at each other. George Cooper raised his hands, as if to surrender. "We don't mean to cause you no harm. We just came for what's lawfully ours. Put the rifle down and look at these papers. You'll see that we ain't looking for trouble. We aim to collect our property and go along peacefully."

The Major clenched his jaw and set his thin lips in a straight line, gesturing for Alonzo to get the papers for him. He kept his rifle pointed directly at them.

"Tell me what it says, son. I don't want to take my eyes off these thieving rascals."

When the Major said "son," Wallace and Cooper both rolled their eyes, then smiled meekly. They were almost friendly when they gave Alonzo a bundle of documents.

"This seems to be a bill of sale to a Phillip Wallace for a male slave named Ben," said Alonzo. "It's dated and signed and has some kind of seal on it. The other paper is a newspaper clipping, describing Ben as a runaway and offering a reward for his capture."

Alonzo lowered his voice and turned away from the strangers. "How do we know that they're after our Ben?"

"Good question, son," said the Major. And then louder, he asked, "What makes you think the man staying with us is the one listed in these papers?"

Cooper dismounted from his black horse and walked stiffly forward. He looked directly at the Major's rifle and then fearlessly into his eyes.

"Our Ben ran off after we sold his son and a couple other younguns' to a farm further south of us," he said calmly. "We hated to let them go, but we needed the money for seed in the spring. Crops were so bad last year we had a time just keeping the family fed. Ben's boy, a big strong ten-year-old called Willie, turned up missing, too, and we heard that the two of them were looking for work in Indiana and up by Fort Detroit where they had that bad fire last year. A couple trappers said they left him off here with you. We don't want no trouble. We just want what's ours."

Major Carter lowered his rifle. "I don't hold with slave trading."

Cooper nodded, his hands open in front of him. "I know that you do things differently here. But your ways ain't our ways."

"Let us talk to him," shouted Wallace, his gray horse prancing impatiently. "You'll see right away that he belongs with us. We've always treated him well. We were wrong to sell his boy and we'd be willing to take them both back and keep the family together, no questions asked, no punishments."

"His boy's not here," said the Major. "Ben said that he drowned in the same storm that nearly killed him. He's just plain lucky to be alive. I can't see how he's any use to you. He can hardly even walk."

"What did you do to him?" asked the quick-tempered Wallace.

"Do to him? Why you..." Carter raised his rifle again.

"We saved his life, that's what," shouted Alonzo, too outraged to keep quiet.

"His life?" asked Cooper, his reddened face clearly concerned.

"I was here when those trappers brought him in," said Alonzo. "He was half-starved and frozen, his feet practically rotted off. He's still big and strong, all right, but he won't be able to do the kind of work he used to do."

"My wife nursed him back to health and we've been giving him room and board these last eight months. Are you willing to pay for his lodging and care?"

The strangers looked at each other and then back at the Major. "We'll make good on whatever he owes. But first we want to see him for ourselves. We want to talk to him," snarled Wallace.

Major Carter nodded. "That's fair enough. But I'm warning you. Ben won't go anywhere with anyone unless it's of his own choosing." He nodded to Adolphus and Amos Spafford who were watching from the path that served as a road between their cabins.

"You can get lodging with the Spaffords tonight. I'll

send Alonzo over with word about where you can talk to Ben, *if* he wants to talk to you, that is. You won't meet face-to-face and you won't meet with him alone. And at the first sign of trickery, I'll shoot your ears off as a warning to everyone that anything you have to say is not worth listening to."

Major Carter stomped off to the barn, but Alonzo stayed and watched the Kentucky men return to Spafford's cabin. *This can't happen! Ben should own himself, same as anyone else.*

He vividly recalled the day of the eclipse when Ben blocked the snake attack. And then, as he did every day, Alonzo thought about Henry. He remembered how Henry had bragged about being the first one that Ben would talk to and how there seemed to be a special understanding between them. He realized that Ben had been as upset as anyone when Henry disappeared.

We've been like family to him this summer – and Ben saved my life! What do you want us to do, Henry? Give us a sign, little brother. Show us what we should do....

8

ESCAPE

Alonzo could hardly believe it! Ben *wanted* to meet with his Kentucky masters.

"Bein' free ain't worth nothin' without my Willy," he said when Alonzo and the Major told him about the strangers' demands. "My woman still be back there in Kentucky. Maybe my baby, too."

"You don't have to go back," said Major Carter. "I can raise the price of your lodging so much that they won't be able to pay. We'll fix it so that they never even see you."

Ben shook his head sadly. "I was hopin' to get settled and then somehow, get my family free. But free men got to work to live, an' with my feet so bad, who'd hire me?" He gazed steadily at the Major and lowered his voice. "It ain't right to go on livin' here. Ya'll been feedin' me long enough. I can't be eatin' no more a' your food."

"You can stay as long as you like, isn't that right, Father?" said Alonzo. "We always have drifters and hangers on here. What about those two New Yorkers, John Thompson and James Geer? They've been with us since August. They'll probably be here all winter."

"Don't they hunt for you?" asked Ben.

"If that's what you want to call the two scrawny bucks they brought in last week," said the Major.

"An' wasn't you plannin' to turn them loose on them stumps in the corn field?"

The Major nodded. "If I can ever get them away from Bryant's still."

"So they be earnin' their way. There ain't nothin' I can do for you once the weather turns cold. It be October already, an' I got no where to go an' nothin' to do."

"That's not true," said Alonzo. "You've been a big help since Henry – well, er, what I mean to say, since Betsey was born."

The Major was still too bitter and angry to discuss Henry's death, but Alonzo knew that his father missed him as much as than anyone. He often saw him staring at the Cuyahoga River, his face drawn and sad, his shoulders slumping. Henry's death had been hard for all of them and not talking about it seemed to make it even worse.

"Didn't Mother say just the other night how glad she was to have Ben here?" added Alonzo quickly.

The Major scowled. "I know what Ben is saying, son. A man's got to make his own way in the world. Ben's used to being the biggest and the best out in the fields, not in the kitchen. But even so, there's no reason to go back with those dirty slavers. After a few more months with us, Ben, you'll most likely be completely healed. Then you can go across the lake to Canada. We lived there the winter before settling here. We could easily get you across."

"Chloe is still there," said Alonzo, brightening. She was Carter's housekeeper during their first months in Cleveland. Her marriage to her Canadian sweetheart was the settlement's first wedding.

The Major agreed. "Yes, son, we could send Ben up to Chloe. We should have done that months ago. Why didn't you tell us you were a runaway, Ben?"

He looked embarrassed. "Ya'll didn't seem to want to know. I would've told you if you'd asked, but why worry Miz Carter? She has enough fears without lookin' for slavers around every corner."

"That she does," agreed the Major. "Especially now."

"How did you get away, Ben?" asked Alonzo.

"It be easy. No slave ever run off before me. The Massa' think we want to live on his farm."

"So you just walked away?"

Ben nodded. "The night they take Willie away, I go after him. It be rainin' hard, an' they don't think to guard him too good. They think those boys don't have no where else to go but along with them. So when they stop for the night, I get Willie while they're sleepin'. The rain wash away our tracks. We be long gone by mornin'."

"It's not too late to run again," said the Major. "We can leave tonight. It's cold, but there's no wind. With you paddling in the back, we'd be well on our way to Buffalo by morning."

Ben shook his head sadly. "That be good a' you, Major, but I ain't gonna' be no more trouble. I see that I got to go back."

"Are you sure, Ben?" asked Alonzo. He wasn't ready to give up.

"It be best."

"But not if they're going to use you wrong," said the Major. "I think you should agree to go only if they mean to treat you well."

"How we know that?"

The Major thought for a moment. Then he said, "We'll go along when you meet with them, and if they try to take you by force or against your will, we'll see to it that they never lay a hand on anyone again."

They agreed that the safest way to meet was to use the Cuyahoga River as a barrier. They decided to hide Ben in the thick brush on the west side of the river and then ask Amos Spafford to bring the Kentucky men to the high ground on the east side. They'd be able to talk across the water and Ben could look at them without being seen.

The next morning, the shrubs and trees glowed with bright reds and yellows in the spot Alonzo picked out for Ben. Typical for October, it was chilly and damp. Ben's nervous breathing sent puffs of vapor clouds up like smoke signals as he sat behind a wall of thick bushes. Major Carter stood in plain sight by the water and Alonzo waited behind a giant water oak next to Ben. Both Carters were armed and deadly serious. Finally Spafford arrived with the Kentucky men.

"Are you over there, Ben?" called Phillip Wallace, his wrinkled face still puffy with sleep.

"Yes, Massa'."

"Where are you? Stand up so I can see you."

"No! Stay down, Ben!" shouted the Major, raising his rifle to his shoulder. "Spafford! Are those no-account slavers armed?"

Amos Spafford chuckled. "Not unless they grabbed some eggs from the breakfast table."

"You agreed to let us meet with him," protested the Kentucky man. "We have a right to see him, if only to make sure he's the one we're after."

"You were sure about that yesterday," growled the Major. "Say what you came to say. He'll show himself when he's ready to show himself and not until."

The shorter, heavy-set man stepped forward. "Ben! It's George. Can you hear me?"

"Yes, sir."

"We're sorry to hear about your boy drowning. Willie was a good boy, big and strong like you. Don't you want to come home with us and get away from all this cold weather?"

Ben chose not to answer.

"Haven't we always used you well?" asked George, his arms outstretched.

"Yes, sir."

"And haven't we always treated you like family?"

"Yes, sir."

"We didn't want to do it, but we had to sell Willie. We had to buy seed for planting. Since you took him away, we had to return that money. But the tobacco crop was good this year. We're in good shape for planting in the spring."

After a long pause, Ben said, "How's Sadie?"

Philip Wallace answered, "She's fine, still working in the kitchen making the world's best buttermilk biscuits. She misses you, Ben. She looks for you every day."

"She know about Willie?" asked Ben.

"No. We just found out. She was hoping you'd both be coming home."

"And what about her girl child, Jemma?"

"She's still working with Sadie in the house."

Alonzo saw that Ben was swaying back and forth as he knelt behind the shrubs. He tugged at the long grasses around him. He seemed to be trying to make up his mind.

"Sadie have her baby?"

"Yes, around Christmas, not too long after you took off."

"Boy or girl?"

"Boy. She calls him little Benny, but it's a bad name."

"Why's that?"

"There's nothing little about that youngun'. Eats like a grown man, already."

Ben smiled and Alonzo knew that he had made his decision to go back. Alonzo stepped forward and shouted, "How do you mean to get Ben back to Kentucky?"

"We were talking about that this morning," said Phillip Wallace. "We figure that it would be best for Ben to ride my horse southeast to the Ohio River at Pittsburgh where we'll hire a flat boat to Cincinnati, then take a wagon back to the farm. It'll be faster that way and easier on us all."

"Is that all right with you, Ben?" asked Alonzo.

He nodded and used the branches to pull himself up. His broad shoulders appeared above the bushes.

"Why, there you are!" shouted George.

"You look same as before!" said the other. "There ain't nothin' wrong with you!"

"My legs be bad, Massa'. My toes done dropped off."

"You just need a little of Sadie's care, that's all," he said with forced cheer, obviously disappointed to hear about Ben's toes. "The sooner, the better, too," he muttered under his breath. And then to Spafford, he said, "When can we get started?"

Spafford shouted down to the Major. "They want to know when they can leave."

"That's up to Ben," he said.

Ben looked at Alonzo and shrugged his slumping shoulders. "Don't matter to me, Massa'," he said softly. "You the boss." His eyes were large and sad when he turned away toward the river.

Alonzo spun around and took off through the woods. His throat tightened as he crammed a fist into his mouth, silencing the rage that threatened to take him over. His head ached with panic. *I've got to do something! Henry would want me to do something!*

And then a plan suddenly popped into his mind. But he'd have to hurry before his father got back to the tavern. It might be dangerous and he was sure that the Major would not approve.

Several hours later, about eight miles south of Cleveland, Alonzo waited with four of his father's horses just off

the narrow trail known as Carter's Road. He chose a spot where the trail veered to the left and then rose sharply uphill. The horses were hidden by dense foliage in a deep ravine, and if he was lucky, they would stay quiet and remain unnoticed.

Two armed men, John Thompson and James Geer, the two New Yorkers who had been hanging around Carter's Tavern for the last three months, waited in the woods at the top of the hill, one on each side of the trail. They had been there for a little over an hour, and Alonzo was beginning to wonder if they had arrived too late. He wasn't expecting to have to wait this long.

At last they heard travelers coming toward them. Alonzo saw Ben riding on a gray horse, George Cooper mounted on a black, and his Kentucky master, Phillip Wallace, walking along beside them. Just as the trio climbed the hill, the New Yorkers leaped out of the woods with rifles on their shoulders.

"Ben, you fool! Jump off that horse and take to the woods!"

Alonzo saw that Ben's face looked shocked and when he didn't dismount, he was afraid that Ben wouldn't allow himself to be rescued. But then Ben seemed to recognize Thompson and Geer, so he slid off the horse and limped into the woods. Alonzo saw George glance at the pistols that were still holstered on the gray horse, and just as he was about to reach for one of them, Thompson and Geer both fired their weapons into the air.

"And don't show your faces here again!" they shouted as they ran after Ben.

"Over here!" hissed Alonzo.

Ben looked like a lumbering bear charging down the ravine. He tripped and fell, rolling until he hit a big oak tree. His eyes were wide as he as he struggled to find his footing, but the hill was too steep for him to balance upright, so he began to crawl as quickly as he could. He kept looking back over his shoulder. The Kentuckians were shouting and cursing and Alonzo expected gunfire any moment.

"Hurry!"

Thompson and Geer ran up behind Ben, half carrying, half dragging him to Alonzo who was ready with one of the horses. Ben grabbed the saddle horn and pulled himself up, swinging his legs up with a long low groan.

"Ride straight into the woods!" whispered Alonzo. "Follow the bottom of the ravine until you get to the Cuyahoga. Cross over to the west side at Tinkers Creek. We'll meet you there."

Alonzo slapped the horse's rump and it took off. Panting and gasping for air, Thompson and Geer untied their horses and leaped into their saddles. Without a word, they trotted after Ben.

Alonzo checked that his horse was tied securely, then crept back up the ravine toward the trail. He wanted to find out what the Kentucky men were going to do. If they planned to return to Cleveland, he would have to think of a way to stop them before his father found out what he had done.

His buckskin coat and pants blended in perfectly with the fallen oak leaves, so he was easily concealed as he darted between the trees. At last he was close enough to hear what they were talking about.

"...not worth it to go chasing after him any more," an

angry voice was saying. Alonzo thought it sounded like Phillip Wallace.

"That's true," said Cooper. "Once slaves have tasted freedom, they're worse than no good. They start spreading the idea around, and before you know it, you've got an uprising. We'd lose our farm without the slaves."

"For all we know, that's the only reason he was coming along so easily..."

"If he wasn't so crippled, it might be profitable to go after him," reasoned Cooper. "We could sell him as soon as we got home. But we couldn't get a dollar for him, the way he is now."

"At least we have his youngun'," said Wallace. "The way that child's growing, he'll be in the fields in no time."

"And we won't have to pay out the reward money."

"And I won't have to walk the rest of the way..."

Alonzo was relieved that they were talking themselves into giving up on Ben. He waited for them to leave, making sure that they were headed south, away from Cleveland and his father. He planned to build a temporary hut for Ben, and then get home before his absence was too noticeable. He'd brought along enough food for a week, but Ben would have to keep a fire lit night and day to scare the animals away from his supplies.

Alonzo had promised Thompson and Geer each a gallon of Bryant's best whiskey if they would secretly rescue Ben. They wanted their payment beforehand, but Alonzo would agree to give it to them in seven days only if the rescue was carried out without injuries, and most importantly, if no one in Cleveland heard a word about it.

"I'd hate to be you if my father finds out that you did something to make his word look bad," Alonzo warned them later during their ride back to Cleveland. "You know how he is. If he makes an agreement, even if he doesn't especially like it, he sticks to it, no matter what. And he agreed to let Ben decide whether or not to go back with those slavers. He wouldn't like it that someone interfered."

"Not even his own son?" Thompson asked.

"Especially his own son," Alonzo said seriously.

The New Yorkers looked at each other nervously. "You got the whiskey, right? A whole gallon for each of us?" asked Geer.

Alonzo nodded. "Gilman Bryant has already set it aside for you. You can get it in seven days, *if* you keep your mouths shut. If you talk – well – if you talk, my father will deal with you, and whiskey is the *last* thing you'll be wanting... "

The two men nodded solemnly and rode on ahead. They had planned to arrive back at different times. Alonzo wasn't sure he could trust them, but at this point, he had no choice. Considering how much his father disagreed with slavery, Alonzo thought that he wouldn't actually be too disappointed about what he'd done. Unfortunately, the Major disliked surprises even more, so until Ben was safely on his way to Canada, it was best to keep quiet.

9

FREEDOM

Alone and shivering, Alonzo set down his rifle and studied the angular ravines that zigzagged through the dormant forest on the west side of the Cuyahoga. The steep ridges were prominent now that the leafless trees slumbered, their ancient skeletons, black and rigid, blissfully unaware that only a few miles away, settlers' axes challenged their sprawling supremacy. Alonzo wondered how the land came to be so uneven. Were the ravines really carved by an ancient glacier like Master Adams claimed, or was this land once the home of huge moles who dug huge tunnels and made huge mole hills....

It was Henry's birthday, December thirteenth. *He would have been ten today*, thought Alonzo, *and he would have liked my huge mole idea.* Almost two months had passed since Ben fled from his Kentucky masters and now Alonzo had come to finish what he had started that day in October.

His friend, Adolphus Spafford, and newcomer, Horatio Perry, had stumbled upon Ben's hiding place last week after the latest snowfall. While hunting, the boys followed tracks leading to an area that was supposed to be uninhabited. They smelled Ben's fire and easily found his little hut. He fed them lunch and without revealing any names, told about how he had been rescued.

Adolphus Spafford put two and two together and went straight to Alonzo. "I can't believe you'd go against your father like that!" he had said.

"I didn't really do anything against him," Alonzo insisted. "My father said he'd go along with whatever Ben wanted to do, but even though Ben agreed to go back to Kentucky, he didn't really *want* to go. He thought he *had* to go back because of his bad feet."

"What are you going to do? You can't expect him to live in that lean-to all winter."

"I know. I've been lucky that it's been so warm and that all our snow has melted so far. Did you tell anyone?"

Adolphus shook his head. "But I can't say the same for Horatio. Ben didn't mention any names and Horatio hasn't lived here long enough to figure out what must have happened, but he was mighty curious about who was bringing Ben supplies. He asked me a couple times."

"Did you cover for me?"

"I said that Ben was probably trapping and hunting with the Chippewa braves who left their canoes next to the Cuyahoga. We found five hidden in the brush that day."

"Good. Thanks," Alonzo muttered just as Polly flitted around the corner to disturb their privacy.

All along, Alonzo had been worried about how he would smuggle Ben to Canada, but now that his hiding place had been discovered, Alonzo knew that something had to be done right away. He had been waiting to hear from Chloe Clements, their former housekeeper who now lived on a 400 acre farm outside of Niagara, Ontario. The post rider finally delivered the news he had been waiting for. Chloe had just given birth to twin girls and welcomed all the help she could get.

"This is odd," his mother said as she read Chloe's letter aloud to Laura and Polly. "Chloe says that Alonzo should do what he thinks best, that she doesn't care when he does it, as long as it's before the river freezes over.... What is Chloe talking about, Alonzo?" Rebecca and Laura exchanged suspicious glances.

He shrugged and tried to look disinterested. "Did you mention in your last letter that I was wanting to join up with one of the sloops sailing on Lake Erie?"

She looked puzzled. "I may have..."

"That's probably what she meant. Father is always saying how we need a regular cargo route from here to Buffalo..."

Then a kettle boiled over on the fire and baby Betsey began to cry, thankfully ending the conversation. The next day, two brothers, who had been clearing newly purchased land near Detroit, stopped at Carter's Tavern on their way to New York to celebrate their last Christmas back East before returning with their families in the spring.

"How would you like an extra pair of hands for your trip to Buffalo?" Alonzo asked when he brought fresh water into the garret where they were shaving for the first time in months.

"Well now, that depends," one of them said with a smile. "Do these extra hands know how to paddle?"

"Better than any I've ever seen," said Alonzo.

The brothers looked at each other. "These hands don't belong to you, do they? Are you trying to run away from your work here at your family's tavern?"

"Oh, no, sir. My hands are puny compared to the ones I'm talking about. But these hands wouldn't want to be seen leaving with you..."

"We ain't transporting no law breakers – "

"That's right," interrupted Alonzo. "These hands are running away, but have never broken the law, at least, not around here."

Alonzo explained about Ben's dilemma and the need to get him to Canada before the river froze. "Can you understand why he has to be transported quietly?" he asked.

They exchanged skeptical frowns. "How do we know your runaway will help us? We've heard that crossing Lake Erie in December is mighty tricky. Aren't there freezing gales that whip up out of no where? "

Alonzo nodded. "That's why you need Ben even more than he needs you."

"He might make the crossing harder," said the other brother. "And we already have as much weight as we can handle."

"Ben's arms are bigger than most men's legs," said Alonzo. "His feet are crippled, but his shoulders are stronger than ever. You'll need extra weight to keep your canoe steady if a gale hits, and Ben can more than carry his own."

The two brothers reluctantly agreed that they might need help, so they arranged to meet Ben the next day, December thirteenth, at the Cuyahoga River mouth. "We won't say nothing as long as your runaway shows up on time," they said. "But if he's late, we're gone. We mean to be in New York for Christmas."

Alonzo got up early that morning and left the tavern in darkness before anyone else had begun to stir. He paddled south on the Cuyahoga until he came to Tinkers Creek where he beached his canoe and hiked west for about a quarter mile. As Alonzo studied the ravines, he thought about Chloe Clements and that cold and stormy day ten years ago when she had helped bring Henry into this world.

Alonzo had been a proud and feisty six-year-old then, his father's shadow, always under foot, always looking for adventure.

"You've got a little brother now," his father had told him. "He'll follow you like a lost pup. You've got to show him what's right so that when he gets to be a big brother, he'll know what to do."

"You mean we're going to have even more boys some day?" Alonzo had asked.

"If we're lucky," his father had said, laughing and pretending to punch his chin. "And if it's one thing we Carters have always had, it's plenty of good luck."

It was true. Alonzo had always believed in their good luck. Through chills and fevers, floods and storms, terrible mosquitoes, tragic fires, endless winters, no money – through all the bad times, he still had faith that everything would eventually turn out all right. And mostly, it had. But now, with Henry gone and all the problems as troublesome as ever, he worried that their good fortune was all used up.

"*Please* let there be enough Carter luck for one more day," he whispered, his voice strangely dull in the sleeping forest. He picked up his rifle and trudged through the twisted path of a dry creek bed. Ben's hut was on the other side of the next ridge.

"Ben! Good news!" he called when he saw the smoke from his fire. "You're headed for Canada!"

Ben's smiling face popped out of the buckskin flap that served as a door in his teepee-like lean-to. Believing that he might be leaving any day, he hadn't done much more than stuff moss into the cracks between the narrow logs that leaned against a larger center pole.

"It be good to see you!" he said, grinning. "I be thinkin' you goin' to let the wolves eat ole' Ben."

"Have they been coming around?"

"They be howlin' since the first snow."

"We finally got a letter from Chloe. You know, our old housekeeper who lives in Canada now?"

Ben nodded hopefully.

"She just gave birth to twins, so she says she needs help. Her husband has a big farm. I'm sure you can work for them a long time." Alonzo told him about the New

York brothers who were waiting for them at the mouth of the Cuyahoga.

"But they said if you're not on time, they'd leave without you."

"Well, let's go!" Ben shouted as he kicked dirt into his

fire. They rolled his remaining supplies into the deerskin flap and made sure the coals were completely out. Alonzo carried the supplies on his shoulder next to his rifle as they set off over the ridge.

"You're not limping as much," observed Alonzo.

"My legs be better," Ben agreed. He used a walking stick, but still kept up with the long-legged teenager.

"I've been meaning to ask you, Ben. Are you sore at me for stopping you from going back to your family in Kentucky?"

"I be plenty riled at first," he admitted. "But then the hurtin' went down in my legs. I see that maybe I can get work after all."

"Do you think you'll ever see your family again?"

"I got hope. Massa' will be watchin' the farm closer now, but Sadie can find a way to run off, same as me. When baby Benny grows bigger, I'll be lookin' for a way to help her. As a slave, I be nothin' and no good to her at all."

"That's true, Ben. After you rode off, I sneaked back to listen to what your owners were planning to do. They talked about maybe selling you as soon as they got back to Kentucky. Most likely, you would have never seen your family again, anyway."

"I be hopin' and prayin' that I can set them free one day. I was sold away from my mama when I was ten."

"I don't know if it would do you any good, but we've been hearing that the Quakers all across New England and over in Philadelphia have been speaking out more and more against slavery. Maybe they could help you."

"That be good," said Ben thoughtfully. "You been hearin' about anything else, lately?"

"Well, we got word from Connecticut that Moses Cleaveland died last month," Alonzo said. "He headed up the first survey of the Cleveland settlement ten years ago, the same year Henry was born. It seems strange that he never got a chance to come back to the town that was named for him."

"There's a lot a' strange things that happen in this world," said Ben. "In fact, I be thinkin' that most everything in life be a lil' bit strange, that hardly nothin' turns out to be what you think it ought to be."

"It sounds like you've been alone in the woods too long, Ben," laughed Alonzo.

After a brief pause, Ben said, "I ain't been alone all the time. The Major come to see me three times."

"My father?" asked Alonzo. "Here?"

"He bring me a turkey one time, a sack a' corn meal another, and a side a' deer the next."

"I thought I kept your whereabouts secret," said Alonzo. "He must have known about you the whole time. Was he mad about you being here?"

Ben shook his head, his dark eyes shining. "He be proud a' you, Alonzo."

"Proud?"

"He say he know you be a man now, after what you did to help me, all on your own."

"You're joshin' me, Ben."

"No, I ain't. The Major be proud, that's what he say.

He say he would'a done it himself but for his promise not to."

Alonzo laughed, thinking about all the sneaking around he had done during the last few weeks. "He must have had a hard time letting me think I was fooling him. I wonder why he didn't say anything."

"He be waitin' for you to tell him."

"I guess we'll talk about it tonight, once you're on your way to Canada. Now remember, Ben, after you get to the trading post in Buffalo, you have to head north to Fort Niagara. It's not that far and you can probably catch a ride. Then ask for Chloe's husband, William Clement. He'll come for you. I wrote it all down in case someone questions you. The letter is in your supply pack in the canoe."

Preoccupied with their own thoughts, the only sound during the rest of their hike back to the Cuyahoga River was the crunching and rustling of crisp brown leaves. Alonzo tucked Ben's leftover supplies into the bulging pack that weighed down the front of the canoe while Ben settled himself at the helm in the rear. Their eyes met for a long moment before darting awkwardly away.

"You probably won't see anyone on the river, but just in case someone is watching, it's best that I walk back," said Alonzo. "That way, no one will be able to say that I had anything to do with your disappearance. I'll get the canoe from the beach later this afternoon."

"I figure I should thank you and your family some how," Ben said, his deep voice low and raspy. "But there ain't no way after all you've done."

"No, it was you that stopped that rattler from biting me last summer," said Alonzo quickly. "I owed you and paid you back. That was all I did."

"We be even, then, is that what you want to hear?" Ben smiled his widest grin, his eyes brimming with warmth.

"It seems like a fair trade," said Alonzo. "But we still owe you for searching so hard for Henry. You helped more than anyone."

Their eyes met again. "Don't you be frettin' none about Henry," Ben scolded. "He be with my Willie now, an' them two boys is grinnin' an' laughin', same as always, pullin' pranks up in the clouds. They be lookin' down at us right now."

"Do you really think so, Ben? I can't stop thinking that if only I'd gone across the river when I first saw him coming down the hill..."

"Yes, an' the Major, he be feelin' mighty bad about tellin' Henry to get outta' bed that day. But most likely Henry woulda' died anyway, whether he go to the river or not. It be his time to go home and there ain't nothin' that you or your daddy coulda' done about it."

"How do you know, Ben?"

"You got to close your eyes an' see with your heart. Before you know what's happenin', you start to feel close to him. You start to believe that he be just fine an' that you be with him again some day. Your mama knows all about this. She got lots a' practice."

Alonzo looked down to hide his stinging eyes. "I'll

have to think about that, Ben. I'm not sure I can do it, but maybe I'll give it a try," he mumbled.

"No, you can't think about it. You got to feel it. You got to let your heart do the seein', Alonzo, then you got to show the Major how to do it, too. Henry be mighty glad when his daddy's heart start to see him. Yes sir, mighty glad."

"The last thing we need," Alonzo said under his breath, "is for my father's heart to start seeing anything – his eyesight is already sharper than it needs to be."

He looked up and tried to smile. "Henry was happy about almost everything, Ben," he said, his voice quivering with emotion, "But I think he'd be especially happy about seeing you rowing off to freedom like this today. I know I am."

Ben smiled and nodded farewell as Alonzo shoved the canoe out into the river. "You an' Henry ain't the only happy ones!" His booming laugh echoed across the sleeping forest. "No, sir! Not by a long ways! You ain't the only happy ones! Say good-bye to your family for me, Alonzo, and a mighty big thanks, too! I'll never forget ya'll as long as I live... and then some! I'll *never* forget!"

And then, as Ben paddled away in the final leg of his journey to freedom, he began to sing, his gentle voice rising joyfully over the soothing swirls of morning mist.

> *Swing low, sweet chariot,*
> *Comin' for to carry me home.*
> *Swing low, sweet chariot,*
> *Comin' for to carry me home...*

Western Reserve Historical Society, Cleveland, Ohio

Lorenzo Carter was born in Litchfield County, Connecticut in 1767. His father served in the Continental Army and died of smallpox in 1778. Five years later, when Lorenzo was sixteen, his mother married Benjamin Ackley and moved the family to Castleton, Vermont. At age 22, he married Rebecca Fuller and settled down on a small farm in Vermont. He and his family arrived in Cleveland, Ohio on May 2, 1797 after spending the previous winter near Niagara Falls, Canada where his son, Henry, was born. He and Rebecca had nine children, but only five survived to adulthood: Alonzo, Laura, Polly, Mercy, and Betsey. Lorenzo Carter died in Cleveland in February, 1814 and is still buried there in the Erie Street Cemetery.

Yes... but what *really* happened?

That's a good question....

Information about Cleveland's first ten years, from 1796-1806 (spelled as Cleaveland in those days) is not very extensive. The first pioneer families were so busy trying to survive, that they had neither time nor energy to write detailed histories about their experiences. Some wrote letters, though, and a few journal entries were preserved. The most reliable information was derived from official records concerning elections, land purchases, military service, and survey results. These historic documents enable us to have a fairly accurate understanding of what life was like during those early years.

We can be quite certain, for example, about the births and deaths of Lorenzo and Rebecca Carter's children. The historian Gertrude Van Rensselaer Wickham found this information written in the Carter family Bible. She also carefully researched the facts about Major Carter that are listed beneath his picture on page 102. Alonzo and Laura, as adults, both documented stories from their childhood.

Eighteenth century historians wrote about the problems with malaria, referred to as ague in those days, as well as facts about the various Ohio Indian tribes, climate conditions, the 1806 landslide, the June 17 solar eclipse, problems with wolves and rattlers, fur trading, and other events protrayed in this book. Official records mention all the book's characters (except Ben's son, Willie - that name was made up) but there were some unexplained mysteries that required educated guesswork to piece together what may have happened, particularly regarding the character, Ben.

Several historians described the tragic death of his four traveling companions, the serious frostbite he suffered, and the unsuccessful attempt of his Kentucky masters to claim him, but none of these accounts explained *why* he was on Lake Erie, *why* he ran away from Kentucky, or *why* he agreed to go back. Some speculated that he probably ended up in Canada, but there is no documentation to prove it.

Another area of historic dispute involves the schoolhouse. Some historians claim a new schoolhouse cabin was built close to Lake Erie in 1806 (an illustration of it was published on page 521 in *History of Cleveland* by Samuel Orth), but others say that the school was probably located closer to Newburgh since more school age children lived there. Official records show that Asael Adams was employed as a teacher in 1806, but not until October. His starting date was changed to March in this book.

Libraries, museums, and working pioneer farms are wonderful places to find out more about history. Lorenzo Carter's family was selected for this book because it was so influential in the settlement of Cleveland. But fascinating stories exist in all families, just waiting to be discovered. All it takes to get started is one good question, such as:

Yes, but what *really* happened?

Purchase extra copies of *Carry Me Home Cuyahoga* (**ISBN 0-9628769-7-6 paperback $9.95**) or (**ISBN 0-9628769-8-4 hard cover $16.95**) or any of these other popular books by Christine Petrell Kallevig at your favorite bookstore, or simply use this coupon to order directly from the publisher. *(Library patrons: please photocopy.)*

All About Pockets: Storytime Activities for Early Childhood - 128 pages of stories, rhymes, games, riddles and songs, all using the popular and practical pocket prop. Ideal for use in educational and storytelling settings. ISBN 0-9628769-6-8 $9.95

Folding Stories: Storytelling and Origami Together As One - 9 short stories for all ages are illustrated by 9 easy origami models. Prefold the paper models for carefree presentations. Recommended for storytellers, activity therapists, teachers, paperfolders, and recreation leaders. ISBN 0-9628769-0-9 $11.50

Holiday Folding Stories: Storytelling and Origami Together For Holiday Fun - 9 original stories for all ages are illustrated by 9 easy origami models. Includes Columbus Day, Halloween, Thanksgiving, Hanukkah, Christmas, Valentine's Day, Easter, May Day, and Mother's Day. ISBN 0-9628769-1-7. $11.50

Bible Folding Stories: Old Testament Stories and Paperfolding Together As One - 9 favorite Old Testament stories are retold with simplicity

name_____
address_____
_____
city/state_____
zip code_____
Please send me:

Qty.	ISBN number	Price	Total

	SUBTOTAL	
Ohio residents add 7% sales tax		
Freight/Handling: Add $2 (1st book), $1 @additional book		
US dollars only TOTAL ENCLOSED		

Write checks to:
Storytime Ink International
Mail to:
Storytime Ink International
P. O. Box 470505
Broadview Hts., OH 44147-0505

Questions? Call 216-838-4881
Allow 2-4 weeks for delivery.

and combined with easy paper crafts. Biblical text is paired with paperfolding steps, making learning fun and effective. Approved for all Judeo-Christian faiths. Recommended for groups of all ages. ISBN 0-9628769-4-1. $11.50

105